The Optimists

ALSO BY BRIAN PLATZER

Bed-Stuy Is Burning

The Body Politic

Taking the Stress Out of Homework

The Optimists

A Novel

Brian Platzer

LITTLE, BROWN AND COMPANY
New York Boston London

Copyright © 2026 by Brian Platzer

The characters and events in this book are fictitious. Any similarity to real persons, living or dead, is coincidental and not intended by the author.

Hachette Book Group supports the right to free expression and the value of copyright. The purpose of copyright is to encourage writers and artists to produce the creative works that enrich our culture.

The scanning, uploading, and distribution of this book without permission is a theft of the author's intellectual property. If you would like permission to use material from the book (other than for review purposes), please contact permissions@hbgusa.com. Thank you for your support of the author's rights.

Little, Brown and Company
Hachette Book Group
1290 Avenue of the Americas, New York, NY 10104
littlebrown.com

First Edition: February 2026

Little, Brown and Company is a division of Hachette Book Group, Inc. The Little, Brown name and logo are trademarks of Hachette Book Group, Inc.

The publisher is not responsible for websites (or their content) that are not owned by the publisher.

The Hachette Speakers Bureau provides a wide range of authors for speaking events. To find out more, go to hachettespeakersbureau.com or email hachettespeakers@hbgusa.com.

Little, Brown and Company books may be purchased in bulk for business, educational, or promotional use. For information, please contact your local bookseller or the Hachette Book Group Special Markets Department at special.markets@hbgusa.com.

Book interior design by Marie Mundaca

ISBN 9780316576956
LCCN 2025941847

10 9 8 7 6 5 4 3 2 1

MRQ-T

Printed in Canada

In memory of Rod Keating

Death ends all things and so is the comprehensive conclusion of a story, but marriage finishes it very properly too and the sophisticated are ill-advised to sneer at what is by convention termed a happy ending.

— W. Somerset Maugham, *The Razor's Edge*

Teaching is the greatest act of optimism.

— Colleen Wilcox, Santa Clara County superintendent of schools

Contents

Prologue
1

Part I: Clara the Emberian
5

Part II: Clara the Sage
41

Part III: Clara the Elder
153

Part IV: Clara the Optimist
179

Part V: Clara the Archon
211

Acknowledgments
291

Prologue

(May 1997)

Clara held a lit candle in a lantern on her lap. For the Synapse of Induction and Elevation, I dressed in velvet black tie, but the classroom blinds were drawn and the lights were off, so the students couldn't see me or one another. Just Clara, by candlelight. In my left hand was the original Ember scroll, in my right the Palladium Scepter reserved for ceremonies of elevation. In the decade I'd been administering the Ember Exam, Clara was my first student to elevate to Archon.

"In the heart of St. George's Episcopal School," I said, "down the causeway through Ember Land, I welcome you to your fourth and final Ceremony of the Synapse of Induction and Elevation, where, after a lifetime of waiting, we have before us a true Archon, with a score of two hundred out of two hundred. Clara Hightower" — and here I tapped her on each shoulder with the Palladium Scepter — "I salute you, your ancestors, and your progeny!"

Her classmates clapped and hooted.

* * *

"Brava!" I said once the lights were back on.

"My ancestors and progeny would be proud," Clara said.

"Really?" I said.

"Mr. Keating," she said, and shook her head. But then she smiled, so I had done my job.

I understand that *Ember Land, Archon,* and *Synapse of Induction and Elevation* might be hard to wrap your head around. That's fine. It was for them, not you. They were children. And it made sense to them. Especially to Clara. Even if she didn't want to admit it at the time.

It was all an act but none of it was. Or a better way of putting it: I knew it was silly. Its purpose was to be silly. But part of the silliness was that I was entirely serious. So maybe it wasn't silly. I'd dedicated my life to this exam. It was important. To the students and to me. That it was important to the students made it important to me. Or vice versa. We middle-school teachers know the value of being silly in order to be serious.

The point is: I used to be able to enchant fourteen-year-olds into a mastery of composition and grammar. I used to be a magician.

Part I

Clara the Emberian

(December 1987)

In the winter of 1987 I was watching *Jeopardy!* and eating moo shu beef when the telephone rang.

"Hello," I said.

"Hi, Rod, it's Enid." Enid Smeal was a fellow teacher at St. George's. She taught art, and, for a short time, we'd made a life together.

"To what do I owe the pleasure?" I said.

"Liquid gold," Alex Trebek said, "is what Kraft calls this product used in its 'Shells and Cheese.' "

"Jacob is too inside his own head. I blame it on a lack of male company," Enid said. "He needs a positive influence around the house more often."

"What do you have in mind?" I said.

"What is Velveeta," a contestant said.

"That's right," Alex Trebek said.

"Velveeta?" I said. "Is that a real type of cheese? Like cheddar? Velveeta cheese?"

"What?" Enid said.

"Sorry," I said. "What did you say about Jacob?"

* * *

Enid's apartment was one of four on the third floor of a six-story former paper factory on Wooster Street. I hadn't been there since I'd moved out a dozen years before. Enid greeted me smiling. She asked me why I continued to wear a jacket and tie even on a weekend. I bowed slightly, an affectation I had had for years that I could not then and cannot now explain.

"Say hi to Mr. Keating," she told Jacob, who was straining to hide behind her legs.

Jacob looked down to his bare toes, and I scanned the room.

Everywhere crystal animals. There had been a few when Enid and I were together, but now they'd overrun the place. A menagerie of little crystal mice, wolves, giraffes, penguins, elephants, and bunnies were scattered over the tables and shelves, giving the impression that Enid and Jacob lived inside an ice sculpture—an impression exacerbated by the fact that for years Enid had herself been sculpting ice. The blocks—nine feet cubed—were far larger than you're imagining. They didn't fit in the elevator so had to arrive by crane through her large loft windows. She set up a tarp on the floor and hacked at these blocks of ice with her knives and chisels until they looked like giant, grotesque versions of these little crystal animals that apparently never stopped arriving in the mail.

If my memory is to be trusted, Enid had a couple of showings in small but well-regarded SoHo galleries that mounted photographs of the sculptures in various stages of melting. There was real tension in those pieces. They were funny and sad in their own way. Enid had talent.

* * *

Back to 1987: Jacob was five. A thin, pale boy. Translucent, blue-veined skin. Pale blue eyes. Plump lips and a slight smile. Bare feet and tiny toes.

He kept his gaze straight down.

I thought I might have misunderstood the situation. Perhaps Enid had been trying to tell me that Jacob had something the matter with him. Autism or sociopathy. Though maybe the boy was just lonely. Now Jacob and I both looked down.

"Why don't you show Mr. Keating your room," Enid said. When instructing middle-schoolers in art, Enid dressed the part of a school-marm with floral blouses buttoned up to her throat. But at home she wore tight jeans and an oversize men's undershirt.

Jacob took me by the hand in a gesture of such innocence and tenderness that I felt the sting of coming tears, but only for a second. His bedroom was dark, lit by a lamp in the corner. A plain jute rug covered most of the hardwood floor. Jacob knelt by his wooden play kitchen, where he had lined up and organized miniature metal and wooden pots and pans, spatulas and whisks; these were mixed among real, adult-size versions of the same objects. He played in his kitchen. Muttered recipes and ingredients. I sat silent and watched. I grew bored, then fidgety.

"Knock-knock," I said after twenty minutes.

He looked back at where I sat on his bed.

"Knock-knock," I repeated.

"Who's there?" he said shyly.

"Candice," I said.

"Candice who?" he said, his focus back on the kitchen.

"Candice door open or am I stuck out here in the rain?" I said.

He looked at me, blinked, and resumed his work.

It took an hour, all told, for Jacob to pretend to write down my drink order, pretend to pour and serve me an iced tea, take my food order, pretend to make the food, serve me each imaginary course, change my silverware, pretend to wash the fake food scraps off the plates using imaginary water, and ask me if I needed any change after I paid the fake bill with imaginary money.

During all the time he cooked and cleaned, I told him knock-knock jokes. I'm a great believer in knock-knock jokes. Creativity within restrictions. Before knock-knock jokes, there were do-you-know jokes. A famous one around the turn of the twentieth century featured the jokester walking up to someone and saying: "Do you know Arthur?"

"Arthur who?" the someone would respond.

The jokester would say, "Arthurmometer!" and run off laughing.

To be honest, I don't really understand that one.

Another: "Do you know Tom?" "Tom who?" "Tom-orrow I'm going to plant a kiss on your sweetheart!"

By the mid-1920s, knock-knock jokes were everywhere. Guests at parties (think *Gatsby*) told them to show off their wit. Businesses (think AT&T) had customers compete to come up with the best ones for their billboards. Knock-knock clubs formed around the country.

"Knock-knock," I said.

"Who's there?" Jacob said.

"A broken pencil," I said.

"A broken pencil who?" he said.

"Never mind," I said. "It's pointless."

No response.

And like that, every week and sometimes more often, I spent an hour or so with Jacob. Enid, in the living room, chiseled her ice block or sat at her potter's wheel. Her glass of milk was half vodka, but who was I to judge? She was a good mother, and it had been more than a decade since we'd been together. Enid was alone with her son and her crystals, so if she took this time each week to get some work done and drink to excess, what business was it of mine?

Every three or four weeks, I'd tell a joke that would make Jacob laugh so hard that he lost control over his little body and fell to the floor, holding his stomach and crying with joy. That he was so slight and delicate made the laughter seem terribly powerful. The first couple of times it happened, I felt awkward for him. I thought again that there must be some problem with him. But he was five years old. Laughing hard at jokes was presumably something five-year-olds did.

"Knock-knock," I said after a month or two of this routine.

"Who's there?" he said, pretending to scrub a wooden plate. He was squirmier than usual.

"Oink-oink," I said.

"Oink-oink who?"

"Make up your mind," I said. "Are you a pig or an owl?"

He hadn't seen it coming. It was the first time I'd used the *who* as a stand-in for the hoot noise an owl makes. I'd thought Jacob might like this one, and it landed. We giggled and repeated "Oink-oink who," Jacob eventually laughing so hard that Enid came in with her vodka milk to check that no one was choking. She tried to understand but didn't get what was so funny. Her frowns just made us laugh harder. I was in my mid-forties and as happy as I could remember.

(May 2018)

I rarely enjoy spending time around young children, partly because I tend to like people in inverse proportion to their eagerness for approval. Performative people of all ages are too often tarnished by desperation. The difference between cute and cutesy is that the cutesy kid wants everyone to see how cute he is. I don't mind cute, but something in me rebels against cutesy. I gather this is one of the reasons people feel relaxed around their pets. Your cat isn't trying to impress you, so when it makes a silly face, you can enjoy it without feeling manipulated. Though dogs, I'm not so sure. Dogs might sometimes try too hard to please.

At five years old, Jacob was far more of a cat. I liked him because of his lack of desperation. And the same lack of desperation in his mother is what attracted me to Enid during the months we dated, back when she was only a few years into part-time teaching at St. George's. She didn't let school politics—or national politics, for that matter—bother her. She found it tedious to hate Reagan, just as she found it tedious to gossip about our coworkers. She was hard and brilliant but didn't feel the need to advertise any pride she felt in herself or her opinions.

But the very attribute I was attracted to in Enid made it difficult for me to be with her. Enid was not outwardly proud of herself, so she was not outwardly proud of us, so she was not outwardly proud of me. I grew desperate and needy; I began to dislike myself, and I moved out years before Jacob was born.

I've always been needy, just as I've always been ashamed of my neediness. Perhaps young children irritate me because they are competition, consuming all attention. Maybe their eagerness to please irritates me because of my own.

Now, in my darkest, most anguished moments, as I lie in my bed or sit strapped to my chair, when my neck is twisted and I'm in such severe pain that I fantasize about Caroline sneaking up behind me with a carving knife and severing a tendon to grant me some relief, I wonder if the universe — some call her "God" — is punishing me for my ego.

The Italians have a term, *contrapasso,* that I've only ever heard used in relation to *The Inferno*. It means something like "suffer the reverse." The idea is that Dante condemns each sinner by making his or her punishment uniquely appropriate to the sin. Murderers spend eternity in a river of blood. Flatterers are punished for all the bullshit they spewed in life by being forever sprayed with sewage. Fomenters of scandal and division are repeatedly sawed in half. That kind of thing.

So here I confess to craving attention. I am performative. I am desperate for notice. For approval. I, an eighth-grade English teacher, created a world where I could be the king of my own tiny realm. With Caroline's son out of the house, I had her to myself. At school and at home, all eyes were on me as I lectured and performed. And now, thanks to a twist of fate — or, to avoid clichés, thanks to a temporary obstruction in my basilar artery just over five years ago — I am unable to move or speak. I am forced to be silent and still.

Dante, that vain son of a bitch, couldn't have done better himself.

(June 1988)

Jacob's sixth birthday was in early June. The party was to be lunch for eight. Enid made a point of telling me that inviting me was Jacob's idea, not hers. I was touched to be included. During the weeks leading up to the event, Jacob was coy about it. The menu shifted according to his mood, from peanut butter crackers to lobster soufflé. I never knew whether or not we were pretending. In the end, he settled on a one-course meal of smoked salmon on graham crackers, s'mores, cold hot chocolate, and ice cream soup. I arrived early to help set up. Other than the salmon, which Enid picked up at Russ and Daughters, Jacob made everything himself.

And none of his friends showed up.

No, just kidding. Everyone had a wonderful time.

But, Jesus Christ, are five- and six-year-olds repulsive. They didn't even know how to drink chocolate milk. They tilted the cups too high over their faces and held them there for too long. The milk that made it into their mouths bubbled back up over their lips and down their chins. They smashed s'mores into their teeth. Some ate the s'mores first, some the melted ice cream, and no one touched the salmon except for one husky boy who ate everyone else's too. That boy wore a Yankees cap and was so thirsty after eating all that smoked salmon, he drank five or six cups of chocolate milk. Unaccustomed to so much sugar, dairy, and fish, he spent the next twenty minutes running up and down the hallway throwing up.

All the parents had dropped off their kids and escaped, and Enid allowed the anarchy. She sat passively, neither disgusted nor entertained. Jacob wrapped his friends in towels to soak up spilled milk, taking special care to give the biggest, most colorful one to the only girl.

After some time, Enid removed a painter's tarp to reveal a *Happy Birthday, Jacob* ice sculpture. The husky boy in the Yankees cap sprinted to it and started licking, turning his cap backward to get his face in closer, and soon everyone else did the same. Even Jacob, who'd seen ice sculptures before, delighted in it.

I found myself furious with Enid for devoting so much time and craft to something that mattered to no one. She didn't take pictures of it, and no other adults were there to see it. She must have spent the entire night working on it. For Jacob. But Jacob couldn't read. None of the kids could. So, in a sense, she did it for me, but that wasn't the case. We didn't do things like that for each other anymore. It *was* for Jacob, in Enid's pigheaded, nonsensical way.

* * *

Every aspect of the party made me uncomfortable. It was shameless in the sense that these kids were too young to feel shame.

Jacob was ecstatic. His friends asked for thirds and fourths on soup, which he ladled from a second tub of ice cream I'd heated in the microwave.

The lone girl had light, straight hair and pink cheeks. During the happy birthday song, she positioned herself with her back to the bookshelf, looked both ways, then pocketed a waddle of crystal penguins.

"Who is she?" I asked Enid later, though something about the girl's manner made me keep silent about the theft.

"Clara," Enid said. "She'll be in Jacob's kindergarten class. She lives in the building too. Her parents are impossible. They're on the top floor and refuse to get the roof fixed. We're all supposed to chip in but..."

(June 1988, continued)

Here the apartment door swung open and in sashayed small-bodied, well-manicured Richard Kingsley Madison IV.

"Mr. Keating!" he said, because he was my boss and liked to keep things professional between us.

"Richy!" I said, because the nickname bothered him.

I was the only person who referred to Richard Kingsley Madison IV as Richy. He was Mr. Madison to his many partisans, and Tiny Dick to his detractors, who consisted primarily of the young women whom, years before as the new head of school, he'd hired in order to go to bed with.

After he married, he became a devoted husband, and against the advice of his psychiatrist, his lawyer, and his patrician wife, Patty, he handwrote apologies to them. One of the women, still working at St. George's years later and at this point married herself, showed me her letter, and I joined her in being touched by its sincerity and pomposity.

Dear Szilvia, he'd written. *Having now been humbled by real love with Patty, I write to apologize for acting out with you some paltry imitation of the same. I thought of you not as your own person, not as a human being who is the protagonist of her own story, but as a bit player in mine. I was an anus, and I will do anything I can to make it up to you. I'm so sorry. My behavior had nothing to do with you, everything to do with me, a fact which, in and of itself, is unforgivable. I don't expect forgiveness, only that you know I know the severity of my offenses. Forever in your debt, Richard Kingsley Madison IV.*

The man couldn't pass up an opportunity to impress.

Standing in the doorway of Enid's apartment, Richy wore, as he always did, a blue blazer, a white dress shirt, a patterned tie, khaki pants, and derby shoes. It was how his father had dressed, and his father's father, and generations of Kingsleys and Madisons before him. Blue blazers and khakis are timeless — outside of fashion, in the same way that NPR tells me that we white people have long felt outside of race.

"Am I late?" Richy said, preening, laughing at the idea that Richard Kingsley Madison IV could ever be late to anything. An event began with his arrival and ended with his departure. Richy was very short, but he made his smallness look like an aesthetic decision. He was perfectly proportioned, handsome, and he wore his costume well. His pants were nicely tailored to his little hips, and his jacket hugged visibly muscular shoulders. His face was composed of tiny, perfect features: A strong jaw. An aristocratic nose. Deep-set eyes with irises nearly as dark as his pupils, which had the effect of making him appear uncommonly thoughtful. Though older than him by a few years, I was one of his first hires. We'd been friendly at

Princeton, where I was his TA. Despite the name, he did not descend from our nation's fourth president, but he never contradicted anyone who suggested he did. He was the fifth or sixth generation of his line of Madisons to attend Princeton.

The descendants of the original Richard Kingsley Madison were name-rich but cash-poor. It seemed the family had spent all its slaveholding/manufacturing/horse-breeding money in donations to gain Richy and his cousins admission to Princeton. As a tiny dapper freshman, he asked me to go out for drinks, a naked attempt to eke out a passing grade in my section, and that evening, all he talked about was money. He needed it. Needed to earn it, or find it somehow. Quickly and in large quantities. "You might think I have a trust fund waiting for me, but I don't! I don't!" he repeated, drunk but chipper.

When Richy graduated, a second or third cousin of his at Goldman brought him on, but, to Richy's credit, he couldn't stand the work. He lasted three years, during which time he earned his master's at Columbia's Teachers College at night, which he must have done with the foreknowledge that he had a spot waiting for him at St. George's as the assistant head of school. Who knows which St. George's board member was doing what favor for whom. Two years after Richy became the assistant head, his boss—a Grateful Dead fanatic who thought deeply about pedagogy and did not interact with a single student during his thirty-year reign—died suddenly of unknown causes, and Richy was made head.

Do I mean to imply Richy had the head of school murdered? Sure I do, but only in an unfounded, mischievous way. Nevertheless, Richy had won. Thirty-five years old in 1980, he had a respectable lifetime position and was already earning more than two hundred thousand a year.

The school had won as well. For a small downtown independent school to be led by a Richard Kingsley Madison was a publicity coup. *New York* magazine's profile of Richy and his wunderkind counterparts at Trinity and St. Bernard's, a piece titled "The Princes of Manhattan's Privileged Private Schools," included a photograph of Richy in the style of a portrait of Louis XIV. Families from outside the five-block radius just south of Union Square began touring.

And I had won. I was brought in by Richy to teach eighth grade, a job for which it turned out I was especially suited. Richy had a sense that I'd be better at working with eighth-graders than college students. My class was "the crown jewel of our English department," according to Richy, or so he said every time he introduced me to a family on a school tour. That was how Richy spent most of his time: taking potential students and their parents, donors, and dignitaries on tours of our musty brick and marble building on Second Avenue and Thirteenth Street.

"Can you believe he was my teacher all those years ago at Princeton?" Richy would ask his guests, having sought me out in my classroom, known as Ember Land, in order to praise my "brilliant heterodox approaches." He let it stand implied that I'd been an idiosyncratic professor as opposed to a disillusioned grad student and eventual dropout from their PhD program, where I'd met and immediately abhorred the most misanthropic, egomaniacal men and women I'd never imagined might exist. These people were theoretically dedicating their lives to literature, but they loathed reading, and one another, and me.

* * *

The point is that Richy left a lot unsaid. Implied. Assumed. Taken as obvious, even or especially when it was bizarre. He implied I'd been a professor at Princeton. He implied that his office had to be outfitted with a Satsuma vase and a Chippendale desk, because how else could the school recruit families to build a proper endowment? (The endowment! He was obsessed with the endowment. Growing the endowment. An endowment was necessary for recruitment, for prestige, for financial aid, for expanding the K–8 school to include a high school that no one was asking for but that would be his legacy.) It was similarly implied but left unsaid that Richy needed an account with Empire Limousine to ferry him to and from his family's Hamptons cottage each weekend, which was why the day ended for the entire school an hour early on Fridays. The traffic, it went without saying, must be beaten.

Did he try to turn St. George's into a place where he'd feel comfortable inviting his uncles, aunts, and Princeton buddies? Maybe. Did he connect St. George's endowment to his own personal wealth? All signs point to yes. But if I've implied in any way that Richard Madison was a loathsome figure, the characterization was unintended. He was, for one thing, a good boss. He hired good teachers—misfit eccentrics such as myself—put us in positions to thrive, and let us teach what we wanted in the way we wanted. And students loved him. He knew each one's name and hobby. He knew their siblings and parents. He attended all the plays, concerts, basketball and volleyball games; showed up at birthday parties; kept a list of who'd done well on recent tests and sought those students out for a *Brava* or *Well done*. Students literally cheered him when he arrived at Ember Land to show me off on his tours. In his way, he loved his students and teachers, and we grew to love him too. To the faculty, he was lavish with flowers and boxes of chocolates, and though he entertained little, when he did, it was with an originality that pleased us all. He was always flitting about, helping here, guiding there, and he was the first to volunteer his services when needed. He carried desks from one classroom to another. He drank and danced at faculty parties so other teachers would feel comfortable dancing too. He made people trust him and he trusted others in return. He was, quite simply, a good time.

(June 1988, continued)

At first, I figured Richy's appearance at Jacob's party was one of his typical surprise pop-ins, but the way Jacob ran up to hug the man made me think differently. I grew dizzy. The hug had none of the reserve or insecurity Jacob expressed around me.

I understood what had happened: I was only one of two calls Enid had made those months before. She'd felt I wasn't enough for Jacob or that I must somehow be balanced out by a different type of man. Just to be clear, I am not Jacob's father, and Richy wasn't either. But I didn't like that we were set against each other in this manner. While I was telling Jacob knock-knock jokes on Saturdays, on Sundays Richy was taking the boy out ballooning or to polo matches. Enid didn't mention it to me because she knew I'd be jealous, and she knew that such a jealousy would be shameful to anyone who saw it, including myself. She must have tried to stagger our invitations to this party, assuming I would be gone by the time Richy came. She wouldn't look me in the eye.

* * *

Richard's arrival made what had been hectic turn chaotic. He'd brought a present in a gift-wrapped shoebox. Richy held the shaking, yelping package in front of him until someone noticed. I noticed. How could anyone not notice? The box was yipping and growling, and there were holes punched in it. But five- and six-year-olds are idiots, and Enid was distracted.

Finally, the little girl tugged on Jacob's shirt and motioned toward the box.

"Is that for me?" Jacob asked Richy.

"It is!" Richy said, at which point Enid looked, saw, and lost her composure. I laughed out loud. It was wonderful to watch unravel the brain of someone usually so well knit.

"You are not giving us a puppy," Enid said, which drew all attention to them. "We can barely feed ourselves on what you pay me, and now we've got to feed the dog?"

"It's a purebred," Richy said. "It's worth more than... well, I don't know what it's worth, but it's worth a whole hell of a lot. I was dining with Bishop Bennet last night, and his pit bull terrier, Rufus, Son of Simon, just had a litter of these things. He asked if I wanted one before he sent them off to various dioceses, and I said, 'Damn right I do, tomorrow is Jacob Smeal's sixth birthday!' "

"Rufus, Son of Simon, is the bishop's bitch?" I said.

"For God's sakes, Rod," Enid said.

"Sorry," I said. "But you have to admit it's an unusual name for a female dog."

"Isn't it delightful!" Richy said. "Apparently they thought Rufus was male."

"Richy, that makes no sense," I said.

"Happy birthday!" Richy said, tearing off the paper himself, gleefully opening the shoebox, and plopping onto the wooden floor the cutest, most terrified creature I'd ever seen. It was a pit bull that had fit in a tiny box, and now it was running around yipping, eating salmon off the floor, pissing everywhere.

"Happy birthday!" Richy said again.

"Get that thing out of my house," Enid said quietly. The children weren't fast enough to catch the pit bull, which, with salmon in its mouth, was running and pissing, pissing and running.

"Enid!" Richy scolded.

"Rufus Jr., Grandson of Simon!" I said.

"It's bad enough you bring that thing into my house to choke on my crystals, but now on my son's birthday, I have to take a puppy away from him? You do realize that's what you're making me do, right? Rip a puppy out of my six-year-old son's hands on his birthday. Is it even weaned yet? I don't have the time or money to take care of the dog. But you've given my son the cutest fucking dog in the world in front of all his friends on his birthday."

Jacob started to cry.

"I can't keep him?" Jacob said, sniffling and then sobbing full-body sobs, his hands in little fists, his face glazed with mucus and tears. When he rubbed the back of his hand on his face, he smeared snot up to his eyes and hair.

"You see what you've done," Enid said, beginning to suppress a smile. The dog was still pissing and running in demented circles.

"The bladder on that thing!" I said. "How much did you give it to drink?"

"You shut up," Richy said, laughing, gathering up the dog. "Who wants a dog!" he said, and all the kids screamed, "I do, I do!"

"That's my puppy!" Jacob said.

"You can't take a dog away from a kid on his birthday and give it to one of his friends," Enid said. "None of their parents want dogs either, you incorrigible asshole."

"You have to stop cursing in front of the kids," I said, so very, very happy. I thought about adopting Rufus Jr., Grandson of Simon, myself, but I didn't want to live with an animal. It had just been torn away from its family, and now it was going to live with me? Alone in the house for ten hours a day? That would be cruel. And even though I didn't want the dog, I wanted this moment to last. Richy's cock-up and Enid's exasperation.

"I can take it," the girl said.

"What?" Enid said.

"I live upstairs," the girl said. "My parents need a dog to take care of them."

The room was silent. This could work. If the dog lived upstairs, Jacob could share it. It looked so solid, the little thing.

"Can we," Jacob said, "share the dog?"

"You really think your parents won't mind?" Enid asked the girl. It was a crazy question. How would she know?

"My parents don't care," the girl said. "I'll take care of the dog. The dog can take care of them."

It must have been due to the girl's unusual seriousness or calm that none of us reacted as though this terrible plan was terrible. We shouldn't have trusted a five-year-old girl to care for another living being, and dogs can't really be shared, but saying yes made all our lives easier. Was this an early sign that she was special? Or just proof that confidence or competence is innate and not learned? Either way, now Jacob could keep his purebred pit bull terrier without it choking on his mother's crystals. The girl's big eyes and smile radiated joy. Jacob wiped his face.

* * *

In celebration, Richy climbed up on the table to pour chocolate sauce on top of what were now shapeless mounds of melting ice. Tongues were everywhere. Two or three children cried because the cold hurt their lips.

I did my best to comfort the terrified animal. I hugged it and snuggled it up to my neck. I hadn't thought it'd be possible to love so quickly. At the time, I don't think I loved a single living thing. But for a moment I loved that dog and wanted it to find peace. Its tongue licked my nose and eyes. "Calm down, Rufus Jr., Grandson of Simon," I said, stroking its neck. "You'll be okay. It'll be okay."

"Come here, Rufus Jr.," Jacob said. He took the dog from me, put it in the shoebox, and carried the box around with him, letting his friends take turns petting it.

The girl took it from him and brought it into the corner to properly introduce herself.

What happened next defied explanation: Jacob saw the crystals inching out of the pocket of the girl's shorts and seemed about to confront her, but then instead he added to the collection, handing her a koala and three prancing deer.

"Jacob David Smeal, what do you think you're doing!" Enid said, sounding far more like a sitcom mom than herself.

"What?" he said.

"Empty your pockets," Enid said.

Jacob did as he was told. Nothing was in his pockets, as he'd stolen the crystal animals for the girl, not himself.

"Clara?" Enid said. "Empty your pockets, dear."

The kids were mostly still focused on the chocolate and ice. At the time it surprised me that more of them weren't watching the indictment and trial, but it strikes me now that five- and six-year-olds spend a lot of their time seeing their friends be scolded by adults.

Clara didn't say anything. Jacob looked down.

"Clara," Enid said.

Clara's cheeks were getting redder, but she didn't cry the way Jacob would have.

Enid was at the edge of the kitchen, Clara in the corner leaning against the bookshelf. "I'm coming over there, dear," Enid said. "This is your last chance."

Clara calmly reached into her shorts pocket and took out and displayed the penguins, koala, and deer.

"How dare you!" Enid said. "You sneak! For all the meals I've served you, all the time you've spent here, you come into my house and you — "

"I asked her to show me her favorites," I said. "To collect them for me."

I lied. I don't know why I did it. I didn't want to see the little girl yelled at. And more than that, I felt a fondness for her. Her affection for the dog. Her ability to find a solution. Clara was young at the time, impossibly young, but already it was clear she was different.

(June 1988, continued)

So I lied in defense of Clara until she repeated my story.

"He asked me to show him my favorites," she said. "I chose the deer, because I love how they look." Jacob said nothing. He looked at Clara and then at me. He was confused, or grateful, or disappointed.

"And I chose the penguins," Clara said, "because they like the cold. I didn't ask first. Sorry."

Enid regarded the girl, seemed satisfied. "I'm sorry I got upset," she said.

Richy had slipped out. Jacob played with the baby pit bull until it pooped in the box, a runny baby–pit bull poop. Jacob left it then, and I certainly didn't want to deal with that. The box was ruined. The dog was scared. Jacob started to cry again.

I began to clean up plates and cups, but I became flustered. Enid, comforting Jacob, told me to leave. She knew this kind of chaos didn't suit my temperament, and I'm not proud to admit how grateful I was for the permission to escape home for the last couple innings of the Yankee game.

* * *

I visited Jacob a few more times after that, but since we had no birthday meal to plan, our meetings lost purpose and momentum.

The dog wasn't around. Jacob didn't want to talk about the dog. He no longer responded to me with warmth. He didn't laugh at my jokes, and I grew desperate.

"Knock-knock," I said finally.

"Who's there?" Jacob said.

"Europe," I said.

"Europe who?"

"No, you're a poo," I said.

The birthday fiasco—which by any objective account Richy had instigated, and Clara and I had substantially averted—had spoiled the innocence of my return to the Smeal household. An alternative explanation: With the combined accompliceship of a helpless puppy and a morally flexible Clara, Jacob ceased to require the assistance of me, a fumbling, nonparental adult teller of jokes.

In any case, things changed. Enid began to look on me with a renewed exhaustion that was certainly warranted more by Richy's behavior than by mine. And within months, Jacob's gaze, on the rare occasions when we passed in a hallway at St. George's, was the gaze of a kindergartner upon a generic middle-school teacher, which is to say the gaze of a small child upon a potentially frightening but otherwise meaningless inanimate object. Toward Richy, no one's attitude had altered in the least. This quality was essential to the nature of Richy, a kind of reputational impunity that protected him, not unlike the morally indifferent laws that preserved the physical perfection of the antique pagan gods.

A new and mostly boring era had begun. I had ceased my visits to the Smeal apartment, and it wasn't until Jacob was in eighth grade that I would start seeing him again regularly. And only at that point would this story's many inexorable recognitions and reversals begin in earnest — all of them dependent upon Clara. With Clara, Jacob would fall in agonizing love, where he would remain for the rest of his unimportant but largely sympathetic life. For Clara, Richy would risk his heretofore invulnerable reputation. On Clara, Caroline would plausibly but unjustly blame the stroke that cost me the use of my body. And Clara, for her own part, would change in unforeseeable ways the fabric of our whole confusing, doomed postmodern world.

Now, that — as the owl said to the pig — is a hoot!

(March 2018)

I've never begun a novel with more misgiving. If I call it a novel, it's only because I don't know what else to call it. I have no traditional story to tell, and I doubt I'll be able to provide you with a satisfactory ending. *Telos* is Aristotle's word for endings, a term usually defined as "how a life or work reaches its full potential." The telos of a rancher is to raise cattle. The telos of the cattle is to provide nourishment. But Aristotle must have been too busy defining terms to focus on the actual rancher, blistered and gassy, who after driving one herd to slaughter needs to circle back and start on the next. Birth, kindergarten, graduation, marriage, children, divorce, retirement, and illness are all beginnings. Even death ends only one life while propelling others forward. There's no such thing as a destination. There's always more journey.

My brain, when focused, is as sharp as ever. But since my stroke, for many hours of the day it isn't focused. I can't speak. Or write. Or read well. When I try to read, I can't make meaning from the letters. They blur. It's like trying to read in a dream. The letters are there, but they're too difficult to decipher. I can spell, so I can sound out the letters, usually, if I focus. But I can only occasionally make meaning. You're wondering how I'm able to compose words and sentences if I can't read them? My neurologist wonders the same thing.

But don't worry. Just because I've lost control of my body below my neck doesn't mean this book will be a downer. I believe novels should contain jokes. I've long wondered why more don't. *Catch-22* has its funny moments. I recall something about chocolate-covered cotton. But the vast majority of novels that were supposed to be funny—*A Confederacy of Dunces, The Sellout, Tristram Shandy, Portnoy's Complaint*—didn't make me laugh. There aren't enough true jokes in these books. At their best, they contain witty observations or manifestations of the absurd. But nothing's better than a good old-fashioned setup and punch line.

Here's one I like:

> *The plague, the flu, and the common cold walk into a doctor's office. The doctor asks, "What is this? Some kind of sick joke?"*

Dissecting jokes has long been a great pastime of mine, and this one relies on the listener's familiarity with the walks-into-a-bar framework: A horse walks into a bar, and the bartender says, "Why the long face?" That kind of thing. What's wonderful about the sick-joke joke is that the bartender—in this iteration, a doctor—is also familiar with the walks-into-a-bar style of joke and is able to preempt the joke by calling it a joke. Equally important to the joke's success is that *sick joke* has come to mean something cosmically awful. Like if your car catches fire as you're driving it off the dealership lot, you might say, "What is this? A sick joke?" So here, *sick joke* has a double meaning: First, that all those illnesses hanging out together and walking into a doctor's office would be horrific, and second, that the joke is a joke about sickness.

People used to tell me that explaining jokes ruins them. But I enjoy it. Telling people why things are funny can be funny too.

Since I can no longer move my fingers, I can't compose sentences by hand or keyboard, but Christophe Lejeune, a friend who made it big in Silicon Valley, gifted me an ingenious system of sensors and software that allows me to communicate. When I focus my eyes for more than four-tenths of a second on a certain letter on a computer screen, that letter is recorded on a second screen off to the side. It's an exhausting process, but then again, I have nothing else to do.

I can't reread or return to edit what I've written, so forgive me if I repeat myself, but Caroline can read back to me some chunks that I'm usually able to retain for at least the amount of time it takes to begin a new section. That's why you may come across frequent space breaks. They arrive when I lose track of what I've composed and need to take a moment for Caroline to orient me. Then I can get going again. The first five chapters took me six weeks to draft, which isn't too bad when I think about it. Almost completely paralyzed and still rather productive! In all sincerity, and with apologies to Lou Gehrig, I consider myself the luckiest unlucky man on the face of the earth.

* * *

If I seem overly confident that there will be readers of this manuscript, I don't think my optimism is misplaced. I am a seventy-seven-year-old former middle-school English teacher composing a novel by tracking letters with my eyes on an apparatus very few people understand. And I hope to keep this manuscript somewhat of a light entertainment—wish fulfillment, that sort of thing. My expectation is that a publisher can easily let it be known that I wrote this novel while in a wheelchair, unable to read or speak. The very existence of this manuscript is a wish fulfilled. What could be more satisfying to agents, editors, and readers than a cripple telling jokes?

Forgive me. I've been inadvertently keeping you in suspense about the subject of this work for which I've already imagined the publisher and elevator pitch. As focus is difficult for me, I plan to keep the novel limited in scope. It will consist exclusively of my recollections of a student, "Clara," whom I met when she was about to start kindergarten, taught when she was in eighth grade, and reconnected with years later. The only knowledge I have of what happened to her in between is what acquaintances of hers have told me or what she herself has said.

W. Somerset Maugham's line in *The Razor's Edge* is something like "This novel consists of my memories of a man with whom I was thrown into close contact only at long intervals, and I have little knowledge of what happened to him in between." It is this line that made me want to borrow—appropriate, requisition, steal—Maugham's structure. Before starting this project, I knew I needed to write about Clara, but I didn't know how. And then it hit me: I could be Maugham to Clara's "man with whom [he] was thrown into close contact only at long intervals." For these final ludicrous years of my life, this novel would let me be Maugham. Maugham, the writer; Maugham, the doctor; Maugham, whose mother died when he was young; Maugham, who stammered and lost faith in God for refusing to cure him; Maugham, who was obsessed with how young people create meaning for the old.

In terms of my writing itself, I could plausibly enough invent what occurred during the interludes between times I saw Clara and in so doing make my story more coherent, but why bother? I might as well tell it straight. It's a good story, and I'll do my best to make it exciting for you. *You* meaning Caroline, to whom I have long wanted to tell the whole story so she would no longer blame Clara for my stroke, and also *you,* the reader. You — assuming there is a you reading these words who is not Caroline.

In theory I am writing to console Caroline, busy myself, and leave something for posterity. But if I hadn't met Clara — or even if I'd met her and she hadn't aced the test that was my life's work — I don't know if I'd have the energy to write at all. I am above all else a teacher, and Clara is the student who made that calling most worthwhile. Who made me feel closest to achieving my full potential. Who let me reach my telos. The Ember Exam is my legacy. And the fact that the student who met its challenge was not only fascinating but also among the most extraordinary people to pass through our lives — that demonstrates the test works. The test and person met and proved each other.

* * *

There is and has always been something about Clara: Her ability to focus on only what she wants to be or feels is true. Her desire to make the very most of her time on this earth. Her influence on how others view their own lives. And it may be that her understanding of human and animal consciousness as well as the peculiar strength and intensity of her character will have an ever-growing influence over her fellow Americans so that, perhaps far into the future, it may be realized that there lived in this age a very remarkable creature. If that happens, you will without difficulty understand who it is I'm calling Clara, and you might come to this novel for reference as well as pleasure.

I call this book a novel, as opposed to a memoir, history, or work of creative nonfiction, only because, by necessity, I'll be forced toward some invention. I don't pretend the conversations as reported are verbatim, but it seems silly to paraphrase when I can try to put you in the scene itself. And to prevent embarrassment to people still living, I plan on having fun with the names and to hide people, but not in such an obvious way that if I refer to a man as short and fat, you can safely assume him to be tall and skinny. Maybe the person I describe as short and fat is actually short and fat. Or maybe he is average in every way.

The only additional misgiving I'd like to lay bare before I begin to tell Clara's story is my discomfort in trying to, as an old man, relate the thoughts and conversations that occurred within and around a young woman and her set. I'll avoid slang for the most part because

I'm sure to get it wrong. Just before my stroke, I happened to force myself to slog through all eight hundred pages of Tom Wolfe's *I Am Charlotte Simmons*, and the absurdity of it made me laugh at first and then grow sincerely angry. Eight hundred pages of an old man imagining the sex thoughts of a college girl and the words with which she'd think them? If you haven't read *I Am Charlotte Simmons* and you're able to run, run as far away from that book as possible. Sometimes I wonder if that book is partially to blame for my stroke. Though I'm completely serious, I am of course joking.

A nice, young, good-looking waitress approaches a table of two men and asks them what they would like to order for brunch.

"How about a quickie?" asks one man. The waitress throws his water in his face and storms off to call the manager.

The man's friend leans across the table and says, "I'm pretty sure it's pronounced 'quiche.'"

(This joke is funny because a female server assaults a man after the man mispronounces a breakfast order in such a way that makes the female server think he is making an advance.)

Part II

Clara the Sage

(September 1996)

Eighth-graders are fabulous. Boys are short, girls are tall, and the tall girls discuss the short boys as though they matter. Also, at thirteen and fourteen, kids don't know anything about anything, so they're amazed by it all: lunar phases, Mickey Mantle, Genghis Khan. They're not naive like fifth-graders, nor are they sardonic like tenth-graders. They're interested in the world, have the capacity to understand it, and are trying to figure out how family and art and sex and science and consciousness and friendship and justice are supposed to come together to form who they are as individuals. Eighth-graders are vegetarians who eat king-size packets of sour gummy worms. With great sincerity they love whoever at that moment is the most famous pop star in the world. They read comic books with titles like *One-Punch Jim*.

It was September of 1996 and I was in my classroom in Ember Land running through the attendance sheet for the first time with my new eighth-graders. Jacob's name surprised me. I hadn't realized it had been so many years.

"Jacob Smeal!" I said. "Look at that!"

"Here," a deep voice murmured from the classroom's back corner.

Jacob was tall but hunched down. Quasimodo, Rigoletto, Richard III, the Penguin—a crooked spine is supposed to indicate moral weakness. Though in real life, I've actually found the reverse: People with the best posture tend to be buffoons. Regardless, my point in all this is that I liked Jacob when I met him again as his teacher, or at least I wanted to.

But as I got to know him over the first couple of weeks of his eighth-grade year, I again thought he might have something the matter with him. Autism or sociopathy. The little things were off. He was quiet. Coy. He never raised his eyes to meet mine, never raised his hand in class, even when I gave him time to think before responding. For instance, I said, "So, what are the five types of commas? Alison, please name them, then JuliaPaige, please give me an example of one, and then I'll circle around to Jacob to provide an example of another." Alison easily answered, "*B, I, L, E, S,* BILES: beginner, interrupter, linker, expander, separator." JuliaPaige had no problem following up with "A beginner comma sets off a modifying phrase from an independent clause, like 'Three years ago,' beginner comma, 'I came to New York.'" But when I said, "Jacob?" he replied, "I pretty much agree with Alison." Sometimes he'd answer questions with "I've got nothing to add" or, increasingly, with something nonsensical like "Double goose in your eye," to which no one could have known how to respond.

(October 1996)

Watch him in recess. See Jacob delicate as ever but now tall and coordinated enough to play basketball. See him become bored after only a few minutes, then watch as he wanders off mid-game to chat with a sixth-grader who has been sitting alone thumbing ants on the concrete. Recess is only twenty minutes long and it takes time to arrange the teams. Jacob's leaving means the other players must repeat the process. But they do so without complaint. Watch as Jacob entertains the sixth-grader, playing rock, paper, scissors with him as though the sixth-grader is six years old.

I'm not doing a good enough job depicting him.

Another example: It's study hall and two fellow eighth-grade boys approach Jacob, ask him for help with their chemistry homework. Jacob shakes his head to indicate that the British mystery novel he's reading is too engrossing. This is adult behavior: not having time for one's friends, being engrossed in a British mystery novel. And it should be off-putting to his classmates, or maybe, manifested with a bit more or much less purpose, it could be cool. But with Jacob, it's neither. The boys move on.

Jacob was kind but aloof. Tall, blue-veined. Bad posture. Messy hair. Plump pink lips. Physically all nose and elbows — sticks and angles — but attractive to his classmates. He was smart, unpredictable, silent or uncooperative in class, good at basketball, alternately generous and selfish. He wasn't a leader or a follower. He wasn't distractible as much as he was distant or constantly distracted.

The thing is, I'm not a reliable narrator when it comes to Jacob, because he had an uncomfortable effect on me. Though he was currently in my English class, when I interacted with him, I felt like I typically did around former students.

Even before my stroke, I hated seeing my former students. For a year we'd been so close. I'd been there for Kevin's eating disorder one year, for Renée's parents' divorce another. Jen stayed after school to work with me on her writing one year; at the end of another, Andy said I'd helped him finally like books. I knew all about these people; we mattered to each other for a time, then that time ended, we stopped seeing each other, and we created something like memory safes in which we locked what we'd had.

My ex-students were all over the city. They came back to visit or I ran into them on the street, and all that closeness vanished. Instead of the thirteen-year-old I'd meant so much to, there stood a fifteen- or seventeen- or twenty-four-year-old for whom I was just one of many former teachers. And what were we supposed to talk about? *How's high school? You still playing soccer? Your sister doing well?*

All these years later I still shudder to think about visits from ex-students. What we both wanted to say—*Remember when we meant so much to each other?*—was impossible, so we shifted our weight from one foot to the other, trying to muster up some of that good feeling we used to have.

And it was this same discomfort I felt with Jacob, except I felt it while I was his teacher. Eight years earlier, we'd spent months together during which I was more of a father to him than his own mostly absent actual father. And now we were supposed to coexist in a classroom with me teaching *Lord of the Flies* and him ignoring my questions?

I wanted to say something about my knock-knock jokes, Richy Madison, the birthday party, but Jacob was too tall now, and what would I have said? *Remember when I came around each week for six months and then stopped? Remember when I dated your mom years before you were born? Remember how you used to be a nervous, delicate, imaginative, tiny-toed fanciful child? Remember when I mattered to you?*

(1987)

For most of the year before Enid phoned to ask if I'd meet weekly with Jacob, I was lonely. Bored. Those two terms can be synonyms. I'd long before split with Enid, and I hadn't yet met Caroline. I ate eggs and toast for dinner, or chicken Parmesan on a roll from the bodega downstairs. I drank beer. I watched the Yankees on TV. Mattingly hit six grand slams that season. The only six of his career. I taught. On Fridays I ordered in moo shu beef and watched *Jeopardy!* Teaching didn't feel like enough. I attended a lot of stand-up comedy shows. Being in the audience didn't feel like enough. I signed up for open mics.

Storytelling was the thing at the time, but I wanted to tell jokes, so I tried to combine the two. This was my favorite long joke I told onstage:

> *Drinking tea takes faith. Or at least hope. Tea starts out bad. But you're optimistic. You stir it with a little spoon.*

> *You pour in the honey and the sugar. And it still tastes bad. Big Tea — the companies that manufacture the stuff — they know what their product tastes like. That's why they give it all the fancy names. Orange Blossom. Darjeeling. Oolong! What a wild ride this is going to be! you think. How lucky am I to get a little taste of paradise! So you pour in your honey and stir it up and sip it gracefully and think: Oh no, this is very, very bad.*

Funny, right?

I never got paid to perform. But I liked the cadence of it. Holding the mic. Setups and punch lines. Questions and answers. I tried it a handful of times. One night I was onstage, and people were laughing. For the first time, I felt good in front of an audience whose members were older than fourteen. The jokes were working. I was funny. I had something. Confidence. Timing. I don't know what it was. Another comedian slapped my back afterward. He said I was the man. The audience applauded. A woman wiped tears of laughter from her eyes.

But then I was walking home cold and alone, and so was the audience, and no one had been helped. Not really. For a good eight minutes, I might have succeeded in distracting them from their boredom or loneliness, but nothing had changed. The audience had laughed, but none of them were going to spend the rest of their lives, or even the rest of that night, grateful to me. No one was making any plans to draft an encomium or erect a statue.

I wasn't a comedian. I was a teacher. Teaching was enough. That's how the Ember Exam began. I could write questions as though they were jokes. Setups and punch lines. I understand that asking questions and expecting answers wasn't any kind of pedagogical revolution. But I also started thinking about teaching in a different way. I could gather all the information students should know from English class for the rest of their lives. I could perform for my students in a way that benefited them. Eighth grade was the perfect time to be entertained. To memorize and absorb all the rules of grammar and spelling, all the strategies concerning language, creativity, writing, and analysis. And I could transform all of it into a series of questions and answers that could be a pleasure to teach and to learn. I could perform with the goal of imparting concrete, tangible, enduring knowledge. I could give that to generations of students.

Question 23. What is the camera method?

Answer: Since you cannot write directly about an abstract subject (such as love) without being abstract, you must turn your abstract subject into a concrete topic that can then be described in concrete, specific words. To do this, imagine that you must photograph, film, or video a scene (two people kissing in the park) that illustrates the abstract subject (love). You then describe what your camera would see.

Question 24. What is the jalapeño principle?

Answer: The general flavor, tone, and impression of a description is created by the denotations (meanings) and connotations (associations) of the words and references you use. Using fiery words and references—*flame, spark, burn, hell, devil*—creates a hot description. Using chilly words and references—*ice, snow, freeze, arctic, igloo*—creates a cool description.

Eighth-grade English could be more entertaining than I'd previously understood. The students didn't need to laugh, but they could look forward to coming to class. No longer did joke telling and teaching need to be separate. I developed a pedagogy of joy. I wrote songs, and my students sang along with me. A preposition was—to the tune of "Here We Go 'Round the Mulberry Bush"—"Anywhere a mouse can go, BUDAS and FLOW, BUDAS and FLOW. Anywhere a mouse can go, BUDAS and FLOW, BUDAS and FLOW."

Question 26. In Preppy Preposition's preposition song, what do the acronyms BUDAS and FLOW stand for?

Answer: BUDAS: *before, until, during, after, since*; FLOW: *for, like, of, with*.

Question 27. In Preppy Preposition's preposition song, what prepositions does "anywhere a mouse can go" refer to? Give five examples.

Answer: *Under, over, through, to, between*, et cetera.

* * *

And the classroom itself could be alive. I began sketching depictions of grammatical rules on the walls. Kids volunteered to stay with me during lunch and recess. We ate quickly and then painted. My classroom transformed from room 207 to Ember Land. We painted the Buddha (BUDAS) sitting in front of a flowing (FLOW) river. We painted a mouse going under a bridge, over a table, through a block of cheese.

This was my favorite short joke:

> *What happened to the man who fell into the coals of the bonfire?*
>
> *He was ember-assed.*

(November 1996)

Caroline and I ate eggs and toast for dinner. Or we went out for sushi. She brought home new books from her store, and we read them together and agreed about them or fought, but mostly agreed. I drank less beer. I woke up happy to teach that day's lesson. In between classes I talked with my colleagues.

"Enid's an excellent art teacher from what I can tell, but her kid, Jacob, has something the matter with him," the math teacher said. We were in the faculty lounge, a cesspit of disappointment and rage. Mr. Hopkins was a skilled mathematician, but he didn't like kids. Exactly the sort of man who shouldn't be teaching middle school. He dressed hip, like he was still a grad student. Jeans and an untucked dress shirt, usually. Stylish glasses. On this day in November of 1996 he was wearing a brown kimono. He was tall and thin, like a baby tree that might not be able to withstand heavy winds.

I drank tea and gnawed through a weeks-old cafeteria mini-bagel.

"No more than the rest of them do," I said. I didn't disagree with

Mr. Hopkins, but I felt protective of Jacob. Harry Hopkins was in his late twenties. Closer to Jacob's age than my own.

"He doesn't say things to you or in your class?" Mr. Hopkins said.

"Like what?" I said.

"Like 'Ramble on, Genghis Khan' or 'Double goose in your eye'?"

"What? I don't know, maybe?" I said.

"What do you mean, *maybe*!" Mr. Hopkins said. He was yelling at me now. "Does he or does he not say 'double goose' in class?"

"Maybe 'Ramble on, Genghis Khan' is a lyric in some song," I said. "Maybe 'double goose' is slang for something benign?"

In the corner sat Bruce, our sad-sack choirmaster. He smelled of shrimp.

"The girls are all over him," Mr. Hopkins said.

"Double goose," I said. "Genghis Khan."

"What?" Mr. Hopkins said.

"Nothing," I said. "I didn't say anything."

Jacob continued to slump along in the hall on the way to class. The school uniform—khakis and a white polo shirt—made him look even more lonely or bored. Everything in me wanted to put an arm around him whenever I saw him, but I controlled myself.

He escaped into his next class.

And then he was quiet again. Sullen.

And then, Clara. Jacob was holding hands with Clara.

(September 2018)

Q: How long have you known Genghis Khan?
A: Forever. I remember when he took his first steppe.

(This might be the best joke. Not just the best Genghis Khan joke — the best joke ever written. "Took his first steppe" is an entire phrase that has a double meaning. You see one-word puns all over the place. But "took his first steppe" is spectacular.)

Q: What do you call a Mongolian leader who doesn't believe in himself?
A: Genghis Khan't

(November 1996, continued)

I asked my students to write down a memory they had never thought important enough to tell anyone about. Just the details. What they saw, heard, smelled, felt. Show, the point was, don't tell. Never tell. Write in a way that makes it unnecessary to tell. Nothing is worse than telling. The worst crime a man or woman can commit is telling instead of showing. The dregs of humanity tell, I told them. You must make me feel the scene in the same way you did, I said. You must always show and never, ever, ever, ever tell.

Clara met with me during study hall to discuss the assignment. This was just after the first Synapse of Induction and Elevation. Over the course of eighth grade, the Ember unfolded in stages. Before Thanksgiving, all students who correctly answered the fifty level-one questions on creative writing and grammar became Emberians.

After Christmas break, the Emberians who correctly answered all fifty level-twos on sentence structure and punctuation elevated to the rank of Sage.

Then those Sages who in the spring correctly answered all fifty level-threes on outlining and poetry elevated to the status of Elder.

And it had never happened before, but an Elder who correctly answered all fifty of the level-four questions on journalism, grammatical case, and essay writing, totaling a perfect two hundred out of two hundred, would earn the title of Archon.

I'd graded the first quarter of the Ember with the excitement of watching the first few games of spring training. Everything was fresh. A new season. I knew the kids, but I didn't yet know what they were capable of. The first fifty questions were, if not easy, at least memorizable. As in most years, more than half my students elevated to Emberian. But Clara's answers were perfect. Every word correct, and surprisingly playful.

> Question 40. Is it grammatically correct to say "She's bigger than me"?
>
> Answer: No.
>
> *Clara's answer: No. Instead, you should say "She's bigger than <u>I am</u>." You need a pronoun that can serve as the subject of the verb <u>am</u>. The form is <u>I</u>, not <u>me</u>. (You would not say "than <u>me</u> am." Or maybe you would? Outside of school, Mr. Keating, maybe you're unhinged!)*

* * *

Clara was a tall girl with an oval face, a straight nose, sunny eyes, a full mouth, and the type of infectious joy that people sometimes refer to as charisma. She was neither pretty nor plain, but even in her school uniform (blue skirt, white polo shirt), she was sparkling, vivacious. Her blond-haired best friend, JuliaPaige Peres, new to St. George's in sixth grade, must have seen something in Clara before the rest of us did. Or it could have been that Clara was the only one perceptive enough to realize the new girl needed a friend. A month or two into eighth grade, Clara was smart in class but quiet. It had taken me the first week of school to remember why she'd seemed so familiar; we hadn't spoken alone since she was five years old. Now, sitting across from me, she said she didn't know what to write about memory.

"The problem is, I don't have memories like that," she said.

I sat at my desk in Ember Land behind my Power Mac 6100.

"Like what?"

"Memories that aren't important. Everything I remember feels important in its way."

I'd given this same assignment for years, and no one had ever raised this objection. But she was right. The very fact of remembering a moment from one's childhood makes it important.

"What?" she said.

I told her to write about the crystal penguins she'd stolen.

"How do you know about those?" she said. She looked around and behind her. No one was listening.

"I was the one who covered for you," I said.

"I never took penguins," she said.

"At Jacob's sixth-birthday party," I said.

"I know what you're referring to," she said. "But they were kittens. And then Jake gave me puppies too. And Mr. Madison lied to say it was his idea."

"They were penguins," I said. "And it was me, not Mr. Madison! I lied and said it was my idea. Do you still have the dog? The real dog?"

"Rufus Jr., Grandson of Simon," she said. "RJ."

"You didn't keep that name?"

"I did! He's a good boy."

"You still have him?"

"RJ?" she said. "He's slept in my bed every night since kindergarten. You were there that day?"

"Then that makes sense why you're mixing up the memory. You took a real dog and crystal penguins. You're just conflating them."

"No," she said. "I remember everything we took."

I was certain they were penguins, but it's possible I was wrong.

"You kept on taking them?" I said, and I smiled.

"We needed to. We sold them," Clara said.

Clara's radiant health, her playful jauntiness, her enjoyment of life, the happiness I felt in her, were refreshing. Since she'd aced the first stage of the Ember, I'd been paying more attention to her. She was so comfortable in who she was that she made the other students milling around behind her seem less real somehow, like background players to her spotlit scene.

"Sold them?" I said. "When?"

"Then," she said.

"You were six," I said.

"Jake was six. I was still five," she said. She smiled. "Jake and I were just talking about that party and how everyone threw up. I remembered Mr. Madison was there but we'd forgotten about you. You're the one who covered for me!"

She laughed. I laughed.

"You sold them."

"We sold them."

"Together? I didn't realize you two were close."

"We weren't for a long time between then and just recently. But back then Jake and I spent lots of time together. We took turns walking RJ. Taking him to the dog park, to the vet, to get groomed. Grown-up stuff."

"You did all this while you were that young?"

"Yes. And when RJ napped," she said, "we used to watch TV together. I didn't have a TV and he did, so I'd come downstairs after dinner and watch. Baseball or cartoons."

"Why'd you steal the crystals?" I asked.

"For the money," she said. "I needed money, but I was also obsessed with money. I kept it in my sock drawer. Inside a sock, actually, and I counted it almost every night. Jake and I counted it together. It was for food for RJ. That's how it started, at least. We would try to find the perfect combination of what Jake's mom would miss the least and what we'd get the most money for. We sold them at one of the surplus stores on Canal Street. We got twenty bucks. It was easy. The stores were just around the corner."

"Enid never knew?" I said.

"Jake thinks she never knew. I give her more credit."

"Five- and six-year-olds can plan like that? And walk into a store to sell things?"

"We could," she said. "I did."

"Bring in a picture of RJ," I said.

She took one out of her Trapper Keeper. RJ had his own folder, just as her English and science classes did. I hoped to see something familiar in Rufus Jr., Grandson of Simon, but he just looked like an old dog. Patchy fur and folds of skin around his neck. RJ didn't look healthy. How many years had it been? Eight? What had fit in a shoebox was now a big lumpy sack of broken-down muscles and bones.

"Cute dog!" I said.

"My best friend," she said.

"You're lucky to have each other."

Clara ended up writing about a veal chop she'd eaten when she was eight, a special meal prepared by her father when her mother was going through one of her down times. The veal chop tasted rich, she wrote. It tasted like what a rich child would eat. It was so flavorful and delicious and special that she'd promised herself she'd always remember it but realized a few years later that the details had probably shifted and that she was remembering the memory more than the thing itself. Her essay tracked her own shifting memory from the beginning, the veal chop alone on a plate, to the way it ended up, accompanied by creamed spinach and mashed potatoes.

It was the best piece of writing I'd ever seen from an eighth-grader. I laughed while reading it, hard enough that Caroline asked me if I was okay. We'd been married now for a few years, and I rarely laughed alone. I read Clara's work aloud to her, and she laughed too. I don't remember many other details from the piece except it played with theme and variation and repeated *veal on a plate*. Why was that funny? Maybe because of the repetition of *plate*? Where else would the veal be? Or maybe the word *veal* is funny? *Veal. Veal. Veal.* Or maybe because one doesn't think about children eating veal? Or maybe because why would a young child try to remember veal and then misremember it and then continue for years to remember the misremembering, only to acknowledge the misremembering in an essay for English class?

And maybe it is memorable to me now because, though veal is delicious, from what I understand it is also a grotesque product of bovine torture and infanticide.

Want a memory? Clara seemed to be saying. *Want something that felt inconsequential at the time? Well, how about a story about a calf that was tortured and murdered for my pleasure?*

(January 1997)

Clara began to excel, and not just in English. It's difficult to explain if you weren't there. I'm tempted to use an expression like "everything clicked," but that's restating, not explaining. My best guess is that seventh-grade work can be completed correctly in such a way that an exceptional student seems merely capable, while in eighth grade there is more opportunity to differentiate oneself. Clara was suddenly extraordinary at everything. Math, poetry, French, chemistry, history. She was one of only fifteen Sages that year. She wasn't much of a visual artist, and she didn't express any interest in playing sports, but when it came to academics, she was like a college student taking eighth-grade classes. As we, in our litter box of a faculty lounge, began to realize that she was doing astonishing work for every one of us, we got in the habit of checking in with one another for the latest highlights as though we were following the Yankees on a thirty-game winning streak.

It was late January. I wore my Russian fur hat and my big Scottish galoshes. I chewed my cafeteria bagel and sipped my tea. Enid sat beside me gazing out the window. She was in a good mood. That morning's snow had not yet turned yellow and black.

"She understands the math as I introduce it," Mr. Hopkins said. "Before I explain it or teach it, I mean. The quadratic formula. I've never seen anyone like her." He wore long green slacks and a green sweater. His body was like a string bean with four string beans added for arms and legs and a mushed-up yellow string bean for a face.

"I just love that girl!" the chemistry teacher said. Szilvia Gorog was Hungarian and coached the school's terrible basketball teams. She's the one who'd shared Richy's apology letter with me years before. "I don't think it's so easy for her in chemistry," she said. "Or I might be misreading her affect. I get the sense she is lost sometimes in class, but by the next day she has mastered the material. She has perfect scores on four quizzes in a row."

Choirmaster Bruce, smelling of old seafood, sat in his corner and added, "She sings well. Remarkably well."

It was then that Richard Kingsley Madison IV — his Royal Madness — strutted into the faculty lounge hips-first.

"Funny little man," Szilvia whispered.

"Our leader," I said.

"Should we do something for Clara?" Richy said. "I overheard you discussing her latest accomplishments. At graduation, I mean, if this continues?"

"Maybe," Mr. Hopkins said, while Szilvia said, "I don't think so," and I said, "Like what?"

"Make her the next head of school!" Richard Kingsley Madison IV said. Though the joke wasn't funny and made little sense, we all laughed.

I've found that in social settings, the success rate of jokes corresponds directly to the confidence and clarity in delivery, in indicating that what's coming next is, unquestionably, a joke. Richy continued, "I'd do anything for that girl. She's the model St. George's student. She'll show the world what kind of students we graduate here."

"Our leader," Szilvia said.

"What?" Richy said.

"She's fucking with you," I said.

"Rod," Mr. Hopkins said.

"Double goose in your eye, Mr. Hopkins," I said. "I'm late for a meeting in Ember Land."

(January 1997, continued)

It must have been because my meeting was with Jacob that I'd double-goosed Mr. Hopkins, though I hadn't heard the phrase for weeks. Recently, Jacob had been treating his classmates and teachers with far more kindness than before and even something like respect.

But his work continued to be below his aptitude. On his most recent essay, I'd spent more than two hours on line edits and potential revisions, given him a D and a scathing comment. I can admit now that he had probably deserved a B plus, but he wasn't working hard enough. He left in misspellings and inadvertently repeated words. We'd reached the beginning of second semester, and I felt as though I'd let him down, allowing him to get by without working for it. That had to stop.

We met at my desk, on which sat my Russian fur hat and my Power Mac 6100. Jacob didn't look angry or sheepish, as recipients of bad grades usually do. He looked me in the eye and said, "We both know this didn't deserve a D. You gave *Eric* a B minus."

Eric had been the husky boy in the Yankees cap who licked and sucked Enid's ice sculpture. He'd since slimmed down and was an excellent first baseman, but he was a very bad student.

"Eric shouldn't be telling you his grades," I said. Jacob didn't respond. His expression didn't change.

"It might not be a D," I said, "but it certainly isn't much good."

"But you gave me a D," he said.

"I did," I said.

"My mom thinks you're losing it," he said.

We both started to laugh. I don't know why. Maybe it was just that the tension caused by our inability to discuss the past was now broken. He straightened up in his chair.

"What's wrong with you?" he said.

"What's wrong with *me*?" I said. "What's wrong with *you*?"

As we laughed, something inside me softened.

"Actually, you seem better," I said. "What happened? Did you find God or something?"

"God?" Jacob was lost for a second. Then he said, "Oh, I see. You're talking about my not...saying the same stuff I did in the beginning of the year."

"Your mother told me she thought *you* were losing it," I said.

I wasn't acting professionally with him, but I don't blame myself too much—he was my friend's son, and I knew him.

"I've grown up a bit, I suppose. And maybe everyone else has too. Can't keep on with the same stuff all the time. Gets boring."

I said nothing. A bunch of students had brought their lunches to Ember Land to hang out in the back of the classroom, and most were playing a fortune-telling game that predicted their future jobs, the size of their houses, whom they'd marry, and how many kids they'd have. They squealed with each new permutation.

Jacob said, "Okay, I suppose there is something."

(January 1997, continued)

Jacob told me the following:

"It's no big secret. I thought the teachers knew about it too. I figured at least my mom would have told you. Clara and I are... are dating. We've known each other since we were babies, but we just started dating a few weeks ago. And I guess I've kind of wanted to date her for a long time.

"Have you noticed it? I mean, have you noticed *her.* I don't mean like I'm her boyfriend and I'm proud of her. I mean, I guess I am her boyfriend, and I am proud of her, but she's doing things I've never seen anyone else do before. My mom doesn't like that we're dating. She says we're too young and anyway are more like siblings than anything else and that Clara will break my heart, but even my mom thinks Clara is incredible. And we're not like siblings. I hung out with her when we were little and since then I saw her pretty much just to take care of the dog.

"You've been teaching here as long as my mom. Longer? Have you seen anything like her before? And she wants to hang out with me. That's something, right?

"Before we started dating, I tried to act like she acted. Reading all these books and not caring about what other people thought. Helping younger kids for no reason. Trying to come off as different. I don't know what 'Ramble on, Genghis Khan' and 'Double goose in your eye' mean. They just make people laugh, and then I don't need to deal with them. For me, it takes all this energy dealing with people other than her.

"But for her, everything is so easy. She doesn't care what other people think, but still she wants to do all this stuff that other people just happen to think is great.

"And coming from where she comes from. You haven't seen her apartment.

"Her parents used to be interesting or unconventional, but now I don't know. They're not right. It's not right the way they take care of her. They don't take care of her. I do. I take care of her now. When she starts talking about how her life is going to amount to nothing, how failure runs in her family, I tell her how amazing she is. They don't have heat or hot water at their place, and the hole in their roof is crazy. They just put a tarp over the roof with cinder blocks to keep the tarp from blowing away. She's kept herself and RJ alive in that apartment forever. She trained a pit bull when she was like six years old. She's the best human being in the world. And lately Clara and RJ have been staying at our place. Not in my room because my mother's a puritan, but sleeping in the living room when it rains or gets too cold. Her parents wouldn't take money, and it's not like Mom has money to give.

"So, yeah, I've been hanging out with Clara all the time, and just, like, watching her do normal stuff has been good for me. I mean, we do stuff too.

“But that’s why I’ve been acting more normal. She’s why.

“Can I rewrite the essay? You really gave me a D? You’re not going to put that on my report card, are you? I’m hoping Clara and I get into Stuyvesant, but if not, then these grades are going to matter.

“Thanks, Mr. Keating, that means a lot. The D is ridiculous, but I appreciate your being hard on me. I know I can do better.”

(March 2011)

More than a decade later, over our second pitcher of beer at the Grassroots Tavern on St. Marks Place, Jacob explained another side of their relationship. One that must have mattered to him as much as watching Clara "do normal stuff."

But first, a trigger warning. I fully believe in the value of trigger warnings. I don't think kids are too sensitive these days. I don't think adults are either. We human beings are sensitive creatures, and to pretend otherwise does everyone a disservice. I once taught *Hamlet* not knowing that the father of one of my students had recently passed away. I wish I could have spared him having to relive it. Or—that's not quite right. Reading *Hamlet* is probably exactly what a young person needs after losing a father. But there's no real benefit in adding to the grieving process the element of surprise.

So let me warn you before I relate Jacob's story: If sexual relations between consenting young people is something you are likely to find disturbing, please skip this chapter. You might lose some depth of understanding, but the plot, insofar as there is one, will remain clear.

This is how, at twenty-eight years old, Jacob described his fourteen-year-old self:

"I was doing homework, lying on some gym mats in the small space under the stairs that led up to Ember Land — you know, where people used to throw their coats. It smelled musty, like the church, or maybe that smell was the painted hallways. Thanks partially to how much I loved your class, that was my favorite place in the school, and I hung out there in the afternoons, sometimes to get my work done and not deal with my mom.

"At first, I couldn't differentiate between her footsteps and the plumbing, but then —

" 'Hello?' Clara's voice echoed around the steps. Remember, at this point we'd hardly hung out for years except when RJ got sick or we happened to be heading to school at the same time so we would walk together, mostly in silence.

" 'Hello?' I said.

" 'Jake?' Clara asked in a nervous way but like she knew I was me. Then she came down from Ember Land and was just standing there.

" 'Yeah?' I said.

" 'What are you doing here?' Clara said in an awkward, act-y way that wasn't like the way she usually was.

" 'I'm always here,' I said.

" 'Yeah, I know,' she said. 'I was looking for you.'

"The way she tried to smile made me relax.

" 'You want to walk home?' I said. 'I'll be ready in a moment.' I sounded, in my own head, for the first time in my life, like my father. Around then, I was seeing him like once or twice a year.

"'No, I was just looking for you,' Clara said.

"'That's all right,' I said.

"Clara looked funny. She was wearing white sneakers with her uniform. Her hair was blondish that day, though it usually looked brown. We'd been catching each other's eye when Mr. Hopkins said dumb things or whatever, but we hadn't hung out just to hang out since we were little kids. She had different friends than I did, or maybe it was just that her only friend was JuliaPaige and I didn't really have friends.

"Everything we've been through since, I still think about how she always ran her fingers through her hair whenever she was about to raise her hand in class. Anyway, now Clara played with her fingers in front of her waist. I thought I might be breathing strange. Or maybe that was just the way people breathed. I wasn't sure. She didn't seem to be breathing strange.

"For a second, I thought I heard another set of footsteps coming down the stairs, and I felt relieved, but then I realized I'd heard something that wasn't there.

"'Are you looking at me?' Clara said.

"'No. What do you mean, *looking*?' I said.

"'Nothing,' Clara said. 'I just see you looking sometimes.'

"'Okay,' I said.

"'If you want to, you can,' Clara said.

"I couldn't read the situation. The stairs were made of gray stone of some kind, and the walls had been painted gray. I looked at her a lot in class when I didn't think she would notice, but I wasn't looking at her now.

"'Do you want to see my tits?' Clara said.

"'What?' I said.

"She'd said that in the same voice she'd said the *What are you doing here?*

"Then she goes, 'Do you or don't you want to see my tits?'

"'No,' I said, suddenly harder than I'd ever been at home looking at the *Hustler* magazine I'd bought that summer. I'd practiced buying it a few times but bought gum instead. And then, with one week left to the summer, I bought it. The guy at the bodega laughed like he'd known all along. He threw in a free pack of gum. I don't know why he did that, but it made me laugh too. I hung out there some after that.

"'Why? Are you gay?' Clara said.

"'No,' I said.

"'It's okay,' Clara said. 'Some of the most amazing people are gay. It's no big deal.'

"'I'm not,' I said.

"She stood there again playing with her fingers in front of her skirt like where her belt buckle would have been. I thought of what we'd learned in science class in fifth grade, about fight-or-flight instincts and how animals in stressful situations got ready with all their muscles and nerves.

"I could hear the heating system kick on somewhere around us in the wall. Otherwise there was no noise from anywhere other than my strange breathing.

"'Then why don't you want to see them?'

"For the first time, I considered—really considered—Clara's offer. I'd never seen breasts in person. In the magazine, I liked the one woman with smaller breasts. Clara was like that. I was still lying on the gym mats, Clara still standing above.

" 'Okay,' I said.

" 'Okay what?'

" 'I guess I do,' I said. I thought about actually doing the things I'd seen in the magazine. It seemed impossible. But Clara wouldn't make fun of me.

" 'Okay.'

"Clara took her uniform-shirt thing off over her head.

" 'Here? Not at home?' I said."

I — his now former eighth-grade English teacher — was thinking the same thing. Eighth-graders make out. And in theory, I knew that some must go to bed with one another. But at school? In the stairwell under Ember Land? Even as mature as we all knew Clara to be, it seemed impossible. Perhaps not morally wrong but certainly psychologically precarious.

"She put her shirt back on and we walked home holding hands," Jacob said. "Pretty much ran home together. People talk about how kids are too young for sex, and I'm sure they are, and we probably were too. But in actuality it just felt good. It felt right. It wasn't gross or illicit. It was sweet. And loving. At the time it was just so much fun. But in retrospect, it was loving."

(February 1997)

I don't think anyone knew they were sleeping together. I never asked Enid about it, but I'm sure she wouldn't have allowed it. So to us teachers, their relationship just seemed so lovely and odd—he, tall and apathetic; she, confident and curious. His presence made her more relatable. And her hand in his made his awkwardness seem like evidence of an inner complexity. There must have been some envious mockery among their classmates, but blond-haired JuliaPaige was a staunch defender of Clara, and Clara and Jacob didn't seem to care. They so clearly adored each other and didn't try to hide it, which I'd never seen before in students so young. Eighth-graders in relationships are cagey: proud and nervous. But not Clara and Jacob.

As far as I saw, they didn't spend too much time together during the school day. During recess Clara chatted with JuliaPaige or went to the library to study. Jacob played basketball. They were mostly in different classes, but they kissed casually on the lips when they passed each other in the halls. Teachers told them not to, but half-heartedly. We'd never seen students do that before and felt strange about interrupting what seemed even to us to be some great and mysterious love affair.

(May 1991)

When I look back on my life, with its accomplishments and disappointments, its endless errors, its dishonesties and satisfactions, its joys and miseries, it seems to me strangely lacking in reality. It is obscure and unsubstantial. It may be that my heart, having found rest only in my later years, had some deep ancestral craving for God and immortality with which my reason could not keep up. Meeting Caroline in 1991 and watching Jacob and Clara together in 1997 provided two of the rare moments of substance. Of something concrete, real, and of value.

I met Caroline at a bookstore. She was the manager, and I bought books. I'd always bought books, but now I bought even more. Some weeks I bought books on five or six separate occasions. Caroline was a painter, a pianist, a recently separated single mother of a teenage son. The curve of her neck, her collarbone exposed, the game of expressing interest and then finding myself interested in whatever interested her. She's beautiful now, but my God, you should have seen her then.

And is love worth explaining beyond that? Chemistry teacher Szilvia Gorog once told me she wanted a man with broad shoulders and perfect SAT scores. She found him at a bar when she was twenty-eight and he was thirty-two. They married. Had two daughters. Eventually lost interest in each other.

I felt unrushed around Caroline. I didn't need to keep talking. She felt safe around me. We were excited by and took care of each other. "Please be home from Ember Land by eight," she'd say. "We have guests coming tonight, and you lose track of time when you're grading." We liked listening to each other talk. We liked the taste of each other's kiss. We matched. Married. What a thing. Her son, Henry, was my best man at our wedding. He and I wore matching suits.

(March 1997)

I've casually mentioned JuliaPaige Peres but should spend an extra moment on her, both because she was a good friend to Clara and because she will appear again in this narrative at a key moment in my life.

JuliaPaige was a capable student; she received A minuses through hard work, rewrites, and taking advantage of extra-credit assignments. She was the type of competent, quick-witted, privileged girl who could have spent her time climbing the mountain of social relevance by making other people feel small. Instead, she found in Clara something of a leader and spent her few years at St. George's following her. From what I could tell, JuliaPaige saw Jacob as a fellow disciple of Clara, and rather than being jealous of their relationship, she considered his devotion a sign that she'd chosen a worthy godhead.

I'm exaggerating, of course. Clara and JuliaPaige were friends and could often be seen together in the back corner of some classroom or the cafeteria writing up lists and giggling at the results. Clara, when alone, did not often appear relaxed, but she laughed around JuliaPaige in a way that made me laugh too.

I remember one particular time when I saw Clara show signs of the woman she would become. In order for me to explain Clara's behavior that day, I need to back up for a moment and describe how lunch worked at St. George's. Students ate family-style. A bowl of rice and a bowl of chili con carne, for example, on each table. The girls and boys served themselves, asked one another to please pass the whatever, said thank you, et cetera. There were some additional options in the salad bar in the middle. And there was a rule — a tradition, really, but we teachers on lunch duty acted as though it was a rule — that students determined on their own who was going to clear the bowls off the table at the end of the meal. Richy believed in the importance of creating moments like this throughout the day, times when the students alone were responsible for working together for the greater good. But clearing was an unpleasant task, because by the end of the meal, in addition to the leftover rice and chili, the serving bowls would be filled with milk cartons, discarded plates half covered in chili, juice cups, condiment blobs, and silverware, all of which had to be sorted into various bins and garbage cans.

Another idiosyncrasy of lunch was that, except for when the number of tables didn't allow it, boys and girls ate at separate tables. Teachers had different opinions about this and memories of why segregated eating had originally been implemented. Some said it was what the students wanted, so why not let them have it. Others believed it had something to do with preventing eating disorders, as some girls might not be comfortable taking a big bite of a taco with boys watching. My sense was that, like the rule about who cleared the table, the segregation started for some long-ago philosophical or logistical reason, and now we came to our own conclusions about its purpose.

The day I'm recalling was the first warm day of the year, a Friday afternoon before spring break, and the cafeteria windows were open. The seventh grade sat on one side of the central salad bar, the eighth grade on the other. Both sides had access to the breeze from the large windows that reached from a ledge a foot off the floor all the way up to the ceiling. The windows opened by rotating slightly on vertical central axes, and to prevent accidents, they could open only four inches at most, but with all of them open, we felt as much outdoors as in, at least as much as one could in New York City.

I used to feel a discomfiting sense of potential when the weather first turned warm. It was a good feeling but an unsettling one. That first-day-of-spring frenzy combined in me a desire to embrace the possibilities out there with the fear that I was incapable of doing so. Since my paralysis, I've somewhat enjoyed the certainty that I can never again be blamed for my lack of day-seizing. Warm weather is just warm weather now. Caroline, after she was promoted to general manager of the bookstore, put tables of discounted books outside once spring began. I liked helping her with those tables. She didn't need help, but I'd offered the first time she had the idea and then it became something of a rite of spring for us. That was enough frenzy for me. I didn't want to attend a picnic or parade. And now no one expects me to.

* * *

But back then, in March 1997, the students were bursting with something close to pure joy. Our rules, their clothes, their bodies—nothing was strong enough to inhibit their desire to shout, giggle, detonate into one another. The warmth, vacation coming, the hint of summer. They'd just gotten their third Embers back, and though only Clara and two others had elevated to Elder, nearly everyone did well enough to keep their grades high. A bunch had been wait-listed at their top-choice high schools, so these scores still mattered. Whispers of Trinity, Dalton, Collegiate, and Brearley filled the halls. These names were aspirational and sacrosanct, longed for by all, their secrets shared by the few who'd been accepted. Our uptown masters. Guardians of an aristocracy attainable by just enough students to tantalize the rest.

Laughter exploded and receded before exploding again. Sweatshirts lay strewn about the tables and chairs. Today, the meal was a favorite, chicken fingers with French fries. Students—first divided by gender and then self-segregated according to athletics, academics, and race—piled their plates with food and ate with abandon.

I'd just sat down with my fingers and fries at an empty spot at a seventh-grade table and was tucking my tie between two shirt buttons when I heard the exaggerated howl that students affected when trying to escalate a minor incident into a major one.

I assumed it was the weather and impending vacation getting them riled up about nothing significant, but when I looked over, I saw Clara standing over a boys' table.

Szilvia Gorog beat me there and was looking to Clara to explain what was going on. There were eight boys, including Jacob, at the table. Though the boys' tables were just a couple feet away from the girls' tables, it felt less like Clara had stood up and taken a few steps and more like she'd burst into the boys' locker room. Looking from Clara to the table, I saw that the boys had purposely made the task of clearing more difficult. Strips of breading dipped in ketchup and mayonnaise had been peeled from the slimy chicken leftovers and spread across the edges of the bowl and platter so there was nowhere to hold them without soiling one's hands.

Mr. Hopkins joined us from wherever he'd been stationed. Even though three of us were there, I had the feeling I sometimes had at school that we were missing the presence of someone more important than we were. Someone who should come in to take charge.

"It's not Eric's turn to clear," Clara said calmly. Eric was the husky boy in the Yankees cap who'd been so taken with Enid's ice sculpture and to whom more recently I'd given the B minus. "Eric has cleared every day this week."

"Eric likes to clear," a boy said. Darin. What I remember most vividly about Darin is that he addressed his father as "Father."

"No one likes to clear," Clara said. "It's not his turn. Choose someone else."

When Szilvia, Hopkins, and I discussed the matter afterward, we all had different opinions of whether or not Clara was addressing Jacob. Szilvia had the sense she was talking directly to Jacob. Harry said that she was talking to the entire table as a teacher would, and Jacob was one of the eight at the table. I felt otherwise — that she was purposely excluding Jacob from her admonishment.

What we all agreed on was that Clara stood next to the table and repeated, "Choose someone else."

"It's okay," Eric said. "I don't mind clearing. Really." Clara had drawn attention to Eric's status as a member of the lowest caste of eighth-graders. Her protection made him more of an object of pity and thus scorn. It was a curious misread by Clara, who usually had so much sense. She should have realized it would be better for Eric if she just kept quiet. But for all her gifts, she was just thirteen, and she wanted the world to be a better place than it was. She wanted justice, even or especially if she had to be the one to administer it.

"It's not okay," Clara said. "It's not fair. And they messed with the food in order to make it harder for you." She was standing; the boys were all seated. Darin tried to snicker with another boy, but the other boy pretended not to notice. Their backs were to the windows, and the light coming in behind them made it hard for me to see the scene clearly. Darin's father was a lawyer at one of the white-shoe firms. Skadden, Arps, maybe. I'd overheard Darin a few times that year talking about his family's trips to the Alps, to St. Bart's. He was the first one with whatever the new video-game system was. Recently he'd been showing off his Motorola StarTAC phone, the name of which I remember because a couple of years later, after 9/11, Caroline insisted that we get cell phones, and the Motorola StarTAC was what we bought.

"You're letting your girl talk to your boys like that," Darin said to Jacob, which was met by the same performative howl that had drawn me to the table in the first place.

I wasn't sure what to do, so I said, "Stop it," just as Szilvia asked something about who hadn't cleared for the longest time.

JuliaPaige had stood up behind Clara and was now approaching the boys. In each hand was a fistful of French fries.

Clara drew the attention back to herself. "Eric is not going to clear," she said. "It's not fair." Jacob looked as though he was going to volunteer, but Clara gave him a glance and he stayed silent. "Darin *will* clear today," Clara said. Darin looked up at her, then to the side at Jacob and Eric. "Darin hasn't cleared in a long time," Clara said.

Jacob must have told her about how the boys always made Eric clear.

"Darin hasn't cleared in a long time," Clara repeated. Jacob stood and started to wipe the sides of the bowl with napkins. "Jake, stop. Darin, it's your turn," Clara said.

"What are you even doing here?" Darin said.

It was then that JuliaPaige selected one of the longer French fries she was holding and delicately inserted it into the ear of a boy at the table. He swatted it out. She found another fry, almost as long, and inserted it into another boy's ear. This boy let it stay. JuliaPaige moved on to a third boy. He had what must have been wide ear holes, because JuliaPaige was able to put two fries in each ear, and they stayed! That boy pointed to his ears with pride. Four ear-fries at a time! JuliaPaige pumped a fist in celebration. It'd be too much to say she was an agent of Clara, but she had clearly adopted some of Clara's confidence. JuliaPaige was funny! I'd been teaching her for more than six months, and I hadn't known.

Szilvia, Hopkins, and I waited. Clara wasn't in charge, so we couldn't force Darin to do what she said. But we couldn't allow Eric to clear either.

JuliaPaige returned to her table for more French fries.

"JuliaPaige!" I said, realizing I should have intervened far earlier. As funny as her routine was, it wasn't appropriate for the school cafeteria. "Stop it! And, Darin, please be kind. De-escalate the situation. Please clear the table."

"I can help," Jacob said without rising to help. JuliaPaige hadn't put fries in Jacob's, Eric's, or Darin's ears.

"Darin," I said. But at this point he couldn't comply without the humiliation of admitting defeat.

"I'll do it myself," Clara said.

Clara leaned between and over two boys to grab the chicken platter, which was smeared with ketchup, breading strips, and mayonnaise. We all watched as she walked to the bins, separated out the silverware, plates, cups, garbage, and recyclables.

As she circled back for the next load, the sunbeam coming from the window shone on the ketchup and chicken grease that covered her hands and the front of her polo.

"I'm going to help," Jacob said, standing.

"Me too, sorry," JuliaPaige said, starting to gather the fries from the floor.

Clara had to slide her body between Darin and the window to reach the last of the plates. Her physical proximity to Darin didn't seem proper. Everyone looked down and away.

Clara's left hand gathered knives and forks; her right covered Darin's phone, which was sitting on the ledge by the window. She sent the phone flying out the open window with the finger flick of someone slotting a coin into a vending machine. I heard the faint snap three stories down as well as the muffled yelp of a woman it must have just missed. But nobody noticed except me and JuliaPaige, who stopped smiling. Clara looked up and saw me looking. She continued to clear the table. The rest of the kids in the cafeteria were ready to leave, so Szilvia, Hopkins, and I waited until Clara and Jacob were done, and I dismissed the students to recess.

(October 2018)

Incidentally, it was from this occasion that I created a rule I've tried to live by since, which I have designated the French Fries in the Ears rule. It states: No matter how dire a situation with no matter how much tension or pain, in order for everyone to survive, there's got to be someone putting French fries in someone else's ears. And if ever I look around and there is no one putting French fries in anyone else's ears, then I myself must find a French fry, find an ear, and get down to business.

(March 1997, continued)

"Come here," I said, catching Clara on her way out to recess.

"He's so awful," Clara said, looking up at me. "I can't just stand there and let him take advantage of other people like that."

"That may be true, but it doesn't give you the right to destroy his property. That phone costs hundreds of dollars. And what you did was dangerous."

"I didn't hurt anyone," she said.

"You could have. You had no idea. Out of anger at Darin, you could have hurt a stranger. A little kid, even. Do you know how dangerous that was?" I was stalling, laying it on thick.

"So you're going to tell Mr. Madison?" she said.

"This is serious," I said. "Everything you're working so hard for—all of it could be taken from you."

"How could you know what I'm working for?" she said.

She was right. I couldn't know. And at the time, it didn't matter.

"Whatever it is, it could disappear if you got caught."

She held my gaze. "So did I get caught?" she said.

I didn't know that either. I didn't care about her throwing an asshole kid's phone out the window. Her breaking the rules didn't bother me; I was impressed. But kids will never learn not to throw their classmates' phones out the window if there are no consequences the first time they throw their classmates' phones out the window.

"When I protected you last time, you kept doing it," I said. "You kept stealing crystals."

"I was five," she said.

"I need you to promise never to do anything like this again. You have to learn to control yourself. It's scary how casually you did that. If you can't promise me that and mean it, I am going to tell Mr. Madison."

"I swear," she said. "I promise I'll never do something dumb like that again. I swear on my life, on RJ's life. I'll control myself."

I can see how it might seem as if she was making fun of me or being coy, but there was something defeated in her voice and body language that made me believe her.

"Then go ahead to recess," I said.

"Thank you," she said.

I don't recall ever hearing about the missing phone. Darin must have lost expensive things all the time.

(April 1997)

Before that incident in the cafeteria, if you'd asked me about the class — economic class, I mean — element of Jacob and Clara's relationship, I'd have called it irrelevant; their story was one of childhood affection blossoming into romantic love. They could have been dirt-poor or filthy rich. But from that moment in the cafeteria, I understood that money mattered. Clara didn't like arbitrary or unearned authority. And though power doesn't always mean money, money always means power.

I wouldn't bring up money except that (1) Clara and Jacob were the two poorest kids in the grade; (2) Clara herself admitted to being obsessed with money; and (3) under the influence of Richard Kingsley Madison IV, Clara ended up choosing to attend one of the richest rich-kid schools in the world.

But at the time, I didn't see any of this. Maybe it's because I was poor like they were. Or not poor, exactly, but of a working-professional class. In 1996, I made $38,000 a year, which is probably something like $70,000 a year in today's money, and since I had no expensive habits or kids of my own, that was enough. But Clara's parents were presumably on some kind of disability or welfare, and Enid worked part-time at the school and had to care for Jacob and herself. Though the parent body of St. George's in the 1990s didn't include the hedge-fund billionaires and descendants of multiple American presidents it does now, the parents even then tended to be moderately successful professionals — doctors, lawyers, and magazine editors — in higher income brackets than us teachers.

In kindergarten, Clara and Jacob most likely didn't notice that they were poorer than their classmates, though maybe other kids had nannies instead of parents picking them up from school or playgroups. But by eighth grade, there was a difference between hobnobbing with Rich King Mad in the Hamptons and making pasta at home because pasta was cheaper than McDonald's. For Clara, a movie was an indulgence, so how was she supposed to talk about concerts and clothes?

That's one of my theories about why Jacob was initially so appealing to her. He knew her. Who she was. Where she came from. She didn't need to introduce him to her parents or explain why there was a tarp instead of a ceiling over her kitchen. She could be herself around him, a self she couldn't be around her parents, whom she wanted to leave behind, or even around JuliaPaige, who knew her well at school but couldn't have really understood her home life. And Jacob was tall and smart, handsome in his way. He was someone to bounce ideas off of, experiment with intellectually (lunar phases, Mickey Mantle, Genghis Khan), socially (*Why are Ruby and Vivienne both wearing that all of a sudden?*), and sexually. He was there, and she needed someone to be there. They parented RJ together. She felt safe around him. She liked listening to him talk.

It's obvious why she appealed to him. She was, according to Mad King Rich himself, the "model St. George's student."

They were excited by and proud of each other. They matched.

(October 2018, continued)

A boy asks a rich old man how the rich old man made all his money.

The rich old man looks at the boy, nods, and beckons him to sit down by his chair.

The rich old man says, "Well, son, the country was going through a terrible time, and I found myself down to my last nickel. I spent that nickel to buy an apple. I can still see that apple in my mind's eye. I polished it for hours and was able to sell it for a dime. The next day with that dime I bought myself two more apples, and I did the same thing. After a few weeks I was earning more and more. I started a small business polishing and selling apples. Then my wife's father died and left us six hundred million dollars."

(May 1997, continued)

Caroline wore a forest-green tank top. Our furniture was inexpensive but elegant. And comfortable. Before Caroline, I'd thought elegance and comfort couldn't coexist. We sat together on our elegant, comfortable beige couch. Caroline sighed, reading her novel. I was grading Ember Exams.

"What?" I said. I wore khakis and a dress shirt. I was tall. Still am.

"Nothing," she said. "I'm reading."

"What?" I said.

Caroline turned to me. "Did Clara elevate to Archon?" she said.

"I'm saving hers for last," I said.

"You're torturing yourself," she said. "You've been a nightmare to live with these past few days, and now I understand why."

Her eyes weren't forest green, but they were a brown that did well near green. I'd told her that, and she'd bought more green. That I had influence over her was thrilling. Lentil soup was on the stove. We'd cooked it together. She'd soaked the lentils. I'd chopped the carrots.

"Grade hers now," she said. "You're making us both crazy. She'll do it."

"She might not," I said.

Caroline's fingernails tapped my forearm: one, two, three, four, one, two, three, four.

"Why does it matter?" she said. "Clara will be the same student whether or not she aces your test. And the test will be the same test."

"Neither is true!" I snapped. Caroline removed her hand. "I want her to succeed. And I have dedicated my life — my professional life — to building a course that is different, memorable, that means something special, and I need proof that it works."

"What are you talking about, *works*? It gets the kids to care. They study. They learn."

"Then I guess it needs to do more than work," I said. "It also needs to be able to identify the best. It has to mean something so kids in the future know it's possible. And not just in the future. I want Clara to live the rest of her life knowing she's an Archon."

"You're serious, aren't you?" Caroline said. "Your hands are shaking. Go in the bedroom and grade hers," she said. "I love you. I'll be here."

"I love you too."

Grading Clara's final Ember Exam was like managing a pitcher throwing a perfect game into the ninth. I slowed my breath. The first few of the fifty questions on the fourth and final Ember were easy. We'd drilled them in class a thousand times. They were about journalism:

Question 152. What does *editorialize* mean?

Clara's answer: When a reporter inserts personal opinion or judgment into a news story instead of giving the reader an impartial account of events.

Question 153. What does BARFO stand for?

Clara's answer: Balanced, accurate, responsible, factual, objective.

I graded on my lap desk with my legs up on our bed. The next section was on grammatical case. This was trickier.

Question 163. What do you use the nominative case for?

Clara's answer: The subject of a verb. Example: The dog barked. He left.

Question 164. What is the subjective case?

Clara's answer: Subjective case *is another way of referring to the nominative case.*

Question 165. What do you use the objective case for?

Clara's answer: It has three uses. (1) For direct objects of verbs. (2) For indirect objects of verbs. (3) For objects of prepositions.

Question 166. What do you use the possessive case for?

Clara's answer: To indicate possession. Example: Her dog's collar.

* * *

Again, all perfect, and on and on. By the time I got to question 181, I was sweating. Question 181 was what had knocked out both of the other Elders.

Question 181. What are the special possessive forms of the eight personal pronouns (the pronouns used to conjugate verbs) that you use when no noun follows the pronouns? Provide explanatory examples.

Clara's answer: Mine, yours *(singular),* his, hers, its, ours, yours *(plural),* theirs.

Example: This is my house. (Noun follows pronoun.) This is mine. (No noun follows.)

This is your house. (Noun follows pronoun.) This is yours. (No noun follows.)

I'd been holding my breath. I hadn't realized I'd been holding my breath. I exhaled. Inhaled. She was going to do it, but when I glanced at the following page—the final nineteen questions, all on essay writing—something didn't look right. The answers were longer than necessary.

Question 199. What is an analytical-thesis essay?

Clara's answer: An essay that presents in its thesis the author's analysis of a topic—a policy, event, activity, person, institution, or work of art—in an effort to understand and explain its nature. It seeks to inform the reader about the conclusions the writer has reached as a result of the author's experience and/or research.

This was correct, and sufficient, but she went on.

An example of a thesis of such an essay: The Ember Exam is a test begun in 1987 by Mr. John Roderick Keating. The purported goal of the Ember Exam is to ensure that students are equipped in matters of writing and analysis before they leave St. George's and begin their freshman year in high school. However, the actual purpose of the exam remains a mystery. Some argue it's an ingenious way to trick students into caring about material they would otherwise dismiss as overly pedantic. Others insist it's Mr. Keating's way of seeking out a small number of elite grammarians who will join forces to infiltrate the United States government and form a deep state of philosopher queens.

Question 200. What is an argumentative-thesis essay?

Clara's answer: An essay whose thesis presents the author's judgment of a topic—a policy, event, activity, person, institution, or work of art. It sometimes attacks or questions someone else's beliefs or judgments about the topic. It often argues in favor of a specific proposal related to the topic. It always seeks to convince the reader to take a specific course of action or agree with the author's point of view.

An example of a thesis of such an essay: Because it creates anxiety and contributes to a culture of competition and fear, the Ember Exam should be dropped from St. George's curriculum.

She'd done it.

An Archon.

At last.

(May 1997, continued)

To my surprise and disappointment, Jacob was not accepted to Stuyvesant, Bronx Science, or even Brooklyn Prep, let alone Dalton or Trinity. He would be off to PS 214 in the fall. To no one's surprise, Clara got in everywhere she applied. She was leaning toward Dalton, where she'd been offered a full ride. I thought she should attend Stuyvesant, a marvelous school where tuition was free for all students so she wouldn't feel beholden to anyone, where students were selected because of their scores on a single test as opposed to familial influence, and where she'd be closer to home.

Clara and I were leaving the building at the same time one spring afternoon a few days after her elevation to Archon and before she had to finalize her decision. I told her what I thought: Namely, that she'd be a fool to attend Dalton. That it would either make her feel bad about herself or turn her into something she didn't want to become.

I didn't say what was also true: That she'd found something that seemed, at least from the outside, to be true love with Jacob, and if she attended a downtown school or even a school with a more typical student body, she and Jacob might stay together, whereas that would be tremendously difficult if she attended Dalton.

She answered that I was being obtuse. That schools didn't turn people into anything. That people were who they were.

I told her that she was being naive. The friends she made—the students around her during prime adolescence—might not change who she was but they would change her goals and vision of the world. They might determine whether she became a poet or an investment banker.

"I don't want to be a poet or an investment banker," she said.

"Then don't go to a place like Dalton that will turn you into one of the two."

"Fuck," she said, "you."

No student had ever cursed at me before. I should have confronted her about it—reminded her that she'd promised to keep her baser instincts in check—but it was funny the way she said it. I laughed.

She didn't laugh. It was her life. It wasn't funny to her.

"Just consider what I'm saying," I said.

She chose Dalton.

At recess during the last week of school, Jacob told me that I'd actually had some influence on Clara and that after our conversation, she had indeed been leaning toward Stuyvesant.

It was only after a series of meetings with Richy that Clara chose Dalton. "Mr. Madison told her that going to Dalton was the surest way to guarantee her success. 'The best contacts and education money can buy, and for Clara it'll all be free!' What an asshole."

"Language," I said, embarrassed at how happy Jacob's displeasure with Richy made me.

(August 1997)

Clara and Jacob spent every day together that summer before high school began. They got jobs at the same Foot Locker and worked overlapping but different hours so they could take turns walking RJ. They read books together, watched the Yankees on TV. That was a wonderful season for the Yankees. We were at the beginning of the best run in decades. Jeter, Bernie, Posada, Mariano, Pettitte, O'Neil, and Tino. But also Boggs at third, and Strawberry and Cecil Fielder platooning at DH. There's nothing like watching a baseball team come together in July and August. Twenty-six addicts and juicers with the best hand-eye coordination in the world spitting and grinning like idiot children.

In late August, to kick off Jacob's freshman year with some ceremony, I invited him and his mother over for dinner. Caroline and I were taking some time apart for reasons that have nothing to do with this narrative, and I've never been much of a cook, so I ordered in Chinese food and served beer and orange soda. Enid ate quickly and left. I was disappointed. I'd thought Jacob might head out early to find friends, and I might go to bed with Enid one last time. I was upset with Caroline, and you know how those things go.

It was actually Jacob who stayed behind. Over dinner it had come up that he hadn't seen his father since Easter, and Jacob and I had gotten, if not close again, at least comfortable with each other.

"What is it," I prompted him, filling his bowl with vanilla ice cream and lining up the chocolate chips, peanut butter chips, caramel sauce, chocolate sauce, rainbow sprinkles, M&M's, and large and small marshmallows I'd bought for the occasion.

"I think I'm depressed," he said.

"I'm sorry," I said. I nearly offered him a beer, but I didn't, and I'm happy about that. "Ice cream," I said, nodding to the toppings. "It helps."

He served himself massive portions of everything. Loaded up especially on the chocolate and peanut butter chips. It was wonderful to watch him indulge like he was a little kid again. Or like the little kid he still was. Fifteen is a confusing age in that way.

"Did my mom tell you about me and Clara?" he said.

I shook my head. "I don't think so," I said.

(August 1997, continued)

I have reconstructed Jacob's account of what happened that day partly from my recollection of what he said to me and partly with the help of my imagination, but he and Clara spent that whole long day together, and I'm certain they spoke of more than I can now narrate. Moreover, I'm sure that, as all people do, they not only said much that was beside the point but also circled around and repeated their thoughts at great length.

Jacob woke up on a Saturday a few weeks before he and Clara were set to begin at their new schools, an unseasonably cool day. It had been a dry, unseasonably cool August, so without the threat of rain dripping into her bedroom, Clara had been sleeping at home. But Jacob felt good. The Yankees were playing the Angels at the stadium, and Andy Pettitte was pitching. Jacob called Clara to propose they splurge some of their Foot Locker money on seats in the bleachers.

She usually picked up the phone on the first ring. It was a cordless, and she tried to keep it by her. But this time—"Hello," her father said. He had a meek, shadowy presence in person but a deep voice on the phone. For all the time Jacob had spent with Clara over the past few months, and for all the years they'd lived in the same building, he barely knew her father and didn't want to.

"Hi, Mr. Hightower, it's Jake. Is Clara around?" Jacob said.

"She's in the bathroom," Mr. Hightower said.

"Please tell her to give me a call back," Jacob said.

"Wait, Jacob," Mr. Hightower said. "Clara tells me you've been a good friend to her."

"Okay," Jacob said. "I mean, I've been okay. That's nice of her to say."

"Clara doesn't say anything she doesn't mean."

"Yeah, I guess that's true," Jacob said.

"Can I ask you a question?" Mr. Hightower said. "I'm glad to have caught you."

"Go for it, of course," Jacob said. "Anytime, I mean. I mean, of course."

"Sometimes I can't trust myself on these things, you know. I can't always trust myself to be observant. But it seems like Clara's doing good, right?"

"She's doing great," Jacob said.

"Are you sure?" Mr. Hightower said. "She's happy?"

Clara's father was scared of Clara. Clara's parents were scared of a lot of things. But it was at this moment that Jacob understood that he—Jacob—was scared of Clara too.

"I mean, I think so. She's doing really great, I think," Jacob said.

When Clara called him back, Jacob proposed the Yankee game but Clara said she didn't feel like it. Instead, she'd meet him at noon downstairs to loaf.

* * *

They sat with RJ in the southwest corner of Washington Square Park on a bench overlooking the big concrete hills. That area is grassed over now in artificial turf, and the Parks Department has set up web-like rope obstacles and climbing structures for young children, but at the time, skateboarders used the concrete hills to practice their tricks. In the fifty-something years I spent in and around that park, I never saw a skateboarder stick a landing. Not once. If there's one thing I hope you take away from this novel, it's that skateboarders are terrible at skateboarding.

Jacob and Clara enjoyed lunch like the healthy young things they were, and they were happy to be together. Clara separated the four slices of pizza they'd bought onto two paper plates, and they shared a large Sprite. After chasing pigeons and catching paper napkins, RJ fell asleep. His giant pink tongue lolled sweetly as his lungs inflated and deflated. They nudged him awake and shared scraps of Clara's crust.

They watched one girl—probably an NYU student—teach another how to do the Macarena.

"Go ahead," Clara said.

"Go ahead about what?" he asked, rubbing RJ under the chin. RJ was always wet under the chin.

Just as earlier that day Jacob had realized he was scared of Clara, he now realized that he had an ulterior motive: He'd planned on taking her to the Yankee game in order to shore things up between them before she went off to the land of the Dalton rich and he stayed behind. They'd spent the whole summer together, but by implicit agreement or fear or, he hoped, the obviousness that they'd do anything necessary to stay together, they hadn't discussed what would happen when school began. When she'd commute uptown and he'd walk west. When they'd have different amounts of homework (she far more) on different schedules (hers far more taxing). When she'd want to stay late (in a new library filled with new, richer kids) to avoid her parents. It was already over. He saw that now.

"What's up, buttercup," she said, smiling.

She spoke lightly. He couldn't match her tone. "We spent all summer together," Jacob said. He wanted to die. "What's changed?"

"What's changed about what?" Clara said.

"I love you," Jacob said.

"I love you too," she said. It was the first time they'd said it outside the context of going to bed together. But she said it in a way that felt like she was breaking up with him. He sighed deeply. He drew away from her.

"Then why are you doing this?" he said, tugging at RJ's neck. "I want to die."

"Let's be sensible," she said, knowing what he meant, as she always did. "We love each other, and we love being together, and we'll always love each other, but what's the plan?"

"We hang out," Jacob said. "We make out. We keep doing what we're doing."

"But to what end?" she said.

"I don't see what you mean," he said.

"Don't you want your life to matter?" she said.

"Sure, but—"

"Then don't you see that all the time we spend together can be better spent?"

"Better spent?"

"All the baseball and fucking," she said. She'd never spoken like that before. He didn't know her at all.

"I thought you loved the baseball and fucking," he said, but she laughed because he couldn't say *fucking* like he meant it.

"That's just it," she said. "What's the point of spending all our time acting in the moment for the moment? Like we're animals? Eating and fucking."

"Stop saying *fucking*!" he said. "What are you talking about?" He was angry now. Crying. He wanted her to die too. They were young and full of emotions that were hard to put into words. They'd cried a lot and laughed a lot together. But this was different.

They watched the skateboarders fail to land tricks.

"So what are you going to do," he said.

"Work," she said.

"Work?"

"Study, train, practice, make money, read as much as I can, prepare myself. I keep on being told I'm capable of great things. Every teacher wrote something to that effect in my report card. You saw. I won all the awards. I have to do something. Or else what is it all for?"

"All of a sudden you're vain now? I honestly can't tell if you're joking," he said, though he knew she wasn't joking. "Is this what Mr. Madison has been telling you?"

"Yes, but not just him. I'm repeating what literally every single person in my life has spent the past six months telling me. I'm supposed to ignore it when my teachers and parents and JuliaPaige and you and everyone else says I'm some kind of special person? I'm the world's only Archon!"

"This isn't funny," Jacob said.

"No, it isn't," Clara said.

Jacob was inspired by what he later told me was the first smart idea he'd ever had: "Isn't love what separates us from the animals?" he said. "It's what defines us and makes us human."

Clara thought about that for a minute.

"RJ loves," she said. "Don't you, RJ?" Then back to Jacob: "What are you talking about? Of course animals love."

He looked at her. She was only fourteen, but she was the only person who mattered to him. The only thing that mattered to him. That she was with him was the only thing that mattered about him.

"So that's it?" he said.

"I'm sorry," she said.

"You're sure?" he said.

"I am," she said. "I'm sorry."

(August 1997, continued)

It may surprise the reader that Jacob chose to say so much to someone whom at this point in his life he knew so little. It didn't surprise me. As every teacher understands, if ex-students are able to get past the initial moments of awkwardness, they tell former teachers things they don't tell other people. I don't know why, unless it's that having experienced the intimacy of being scolded, complimented, and moved this way and that, they have a familial feeling toward teachers without any of the stickiness of family. And I think Jacob felt I liked Clara and him, that their youth touched me, and that I was sympathetic to their distresses.

When Jacob finished his story, he looked at me pitifully.

"Do you think I should have done something different?" he said.

"I think you did the only thing you could do, but what's more, I think that you've been fortunate to realize at such a young age that it doesn't matter what's right or fair if the person you want to be with decides she doesn't want to be with you."

He kept silent, spooning his ice cream soup in circles. He was six years old again, imagining who knows what.

"Of course, I know Clara far less than you do," I said, "but isn't it possible she's looking for something but doesn't know what it is or even if it exists? She's fourteen years old, about to attend a school full of the type of people who have always fascinated her but that she has never lived among. And furthermore, whatever she experienced growing up with her parents might have been challenging. My parents weren't traditional parents either. I was alone a lot, and that can be confusing."

"She's not alone a lot," Jacob said. "She's with me. And before JuliaPaige went off to boarding school, they hung out too."

"True," I said. "Sorry."

"And it's not confusing what she's looking for. She wants money," he said. "She's leaving me for money."

Jacob screamed. He screamed in such a way that at first I thought he must be in physical pain. I didn't hug him for the same reasons I hadn't offered him a beer.

When he left, I called Caroline, apologized for everything, told her everything was my fault, begged her for a second chance.

Caroline took me back. In that way, I owe more to Jacob than he could ever know.

(1990)

I don't want to give the reader the impression that I am intentionally hiding some specific trauma that occurred when Clara was younger, a trauma I plan to reveal at a key moment in this novel. If there was some pivotal, life-defining event in Clara's life, as far as I know, she never told anyone about it. Clara suffered from poverty, plain and simple.

Clara did, however, eventually tell a friend of hers — Christophe Lejeune, a cofounder of a data-analysis firm called Bananalytics in which Clara became involved for a period and whom I happened to know too — about an especially difficult moment when she was seven or eight.

Monsieur Lejeune repeated it to me, years later, so I can only relate it at second hand.

Apparently, Clara told Monsieur Lejeune that her mother had what Clara referred to as "down times," episodes where she would be in bed for days, when Clara was growing up. Clara said she and her father just got used to it. But she also said that her father couldn't leave the apartment—he'd developed something like agoraphobia—so her mother worked when she could, but sometimes she couldn't, so they managed as best as possible. If Clara had to steal something small from a store, she did. They never went hungry.

Christophe seemed especially to recall Clara's sense that she was happiest when her mother was struggling the most because that was when Clara's father mustered all his energy. Those were some of her happiest memories growing up, the days when her mother had her down times and her father stepped up. They played cards or chess or they wrestled with their pit bull, but mostly her father read to her from his journals. Long prose poems and thoughts he'd had when he was in his twenties. Fantasies about utopias where people lived in harmony together connected by impossible technology. Clara liked to joke that her father invented the internet in those notebooks.

Lejeune suggested to her that maybe that's what drew her to Silicon Valley. Clara told him to fuck off. Monsieur Lejeune laughed.

One day, Christophe recounted to me, when Clara was seven or eight, her mother couldn't get out of bed. And for a week, her father kept up his routine, baking bread for Clara and reading books and his journals to her. Joking around. Giving her whatever pocket change he found and telling her to go treat herself. But then a week turned into a month and then into a few months, and he couldn't keep it up. He slowly descended into himself again. Clara's mother couldn't be around them. They didn't eat for a day or two.

But lots of kids grow up poor, far poorer than Clara. And lots of kids grow up with parents facing physical and psychological obstacles.

There is no such thing as an origin story. Clara—or I, for that matter—could have turned into any type of person in spite of going, or because she went, a couple days without a proper meal. My point is that villains have origin stories as much as heroes do, and often the same story can serve as an explanation of either good or evil.

(June 1998)

I didn't see Jacob until the following year's eighth-grade graduation, which he attended to support his mother, who was giving the commencement address. Every teacher who'd been at St. George's for more than twenty years was expected to deliver a commencement address and send off that year's graduates with a speech about the students' glowing pasts and glorious futures. I'd delivered mine a few years before.

Jacob sat beside his mother up on the chancel of St. George's church. I sat beside Mr. Hopkins in a back pew. He was wearing khaki pants and a yellow suede jacket. His body was like a strip of banana peel.

"They're wild today," Mr. Hopkins said. "Graduation turns them into animals."

"It's the moon," I said.

"I said they're rowdy," Mr. Hopkins said.

"It's the full moon," I said.

He looked at me in the manner that people sometimes did.

"The full moon makes them wild," I said.

"Come on," he said. "You can't believe that."

"You're a man of science," I said.

He laughed.

"You're a man of science. Tell me what you know about the tides."

"Gravitational force," he said. "Right? They rise and fall according to the phases and the gravitational pull of the moon."

"And what percentage of the human body is water?" I said.

"I don't know. Fifty-five? Sixty?" Mr. Hopkins said.

"For children, it's more than seventy percent," I said. "You're telling me that the moon is strong enough to lift an ocean ten feet up a shoreline but not strong enough to make a thirteen-year-old feel a little bit tipsy?"

"Okay," Mr. Hopkins said. "It's the moon."

We sat in silence for a moment.

"What did the astronomers do when they got sick of watching the moon's revolution around the Earth?" Mr. Hopkins said.

"What?" I said.

"They called it a day," he said.

"There you go!" I said. "Well done!"

(June 1998, continued)

Each member of the St. George's choir dressed in immaculate white. Sad-sack Bruce, the choirmaster, stood resplendent in his flowing purple robes. He conducted the students through "All Things Bright and Beautiful." A glorious song, but the third verse always caught me off guard.

The rich man in his castle,
The poor man at his gate,
God made them high and lowly,
And ordered their estate.

Could you imagine believing in a God that made some people high and others lowly? And I realize that you need that final line to complete the rhyme scheme, but "ordered their estate" really hammers the nail into the lowlies' coffins. This stanza exposes the sinister nature of the entire hymn's class determinism, reframing the first, more famous one:

All things bright and beautiful,
All creatures great and small,
All things wise and wonderful,
The Lord God made them all.

Without the third stanza about God making some men high and some men lowly, I never would have started wondering about all the things dark and ugly, ignorant and dreadful, that God also made.

It's a nasty verse that corresponds too well to the role of private schools, the main function of which is to ensure that the children of the aristocracy retain their position in the aristocracy.

Why, then, did I work at such a place? Because it was a great job. I worked alongside caring, intelligent colleagues and taught students who showed me kindness and respect. I was a good Christian before my stroke. I believed that Jesus Christ was the word of God manifested in physical form on Earth until His Crucifixion. I believed this man was God or this God was a man. And I tried to live as He taught me to.

For the first year after my stroke, I stopped believing. How could a benevolent, omnipotent, omniscient God condemn me to this life? What had I done to deserve it?

But then late one night, as I was trying to draw breath while vomiting a hardened bit of oatmeal that had lodged itself in my esophagus, the answer struck me as obvious. God might be omniscient. He might be omnipotent. But who ever said God was benevolent? In the Old Testament, He frequently takes revenge; He tortures; He kills. In the New, He might be less actively cruel, but He certainly orders the estate of many who suffer. Sure, Jesus fed the hungry and cured the lepers, but before and after He showed up, there were many more afflicted by leprosy and hunger.

Do you know the difference between jealousy and envy? You're jealous about your own possessions. You want to make sure others don't take what you have away from you. But you're envious when you want what others have. So you envy your neighbor's larger house or beautiful spouse, but you're jealous when you see your wife talking with another man.

If you were Clara, you might not have had much to be jealous of, but you were envious of the rich kids who'd gotten into Dalton without even trying while the poorer kids had to compete to get into Stuyvesant.

God doesn't envy. There's nothing God wants but doesn't have. God is jealous. God doesn't want His faithful servants believing in anything other than God. God wants to keep us locked down.

He gave us eyes to see them,
And lips that we might tell,
How great is God Almighty,
Who has made all things well.

(January 2019)

A small church is raising funds for a new piano. On Sunday the pastor says, "Whoever gives the most money for the offering today can pick out three hymns."

So they pass the offering plate around and the pastor sees a hundred-dollar bill in the plate.

He says, "Looks like we have a winner! Whoever gave the hundred-dollar bill can come to the front and select three hymns."

An eighty-year-old lady slowly gets up, walks to the front, turns, and points her finger into the pews.

"I'll take him, him, and him!"

(This joke is funny because a woman in her eighties is lonely and to her it is worth a hundred dollars to purchase the company of men. Perhaps she intentionally misunderstands the offer of *hymns* to mean *hims*, or perhaps she has recently been experiencing a decline in mental acuity.)

(June 1998, continued)

Enid wore her usual teacher costume for graduation: a pleated dress buttoned up to the neck with puffed sleeves. It was pretty for what it was. She looked tired. We were all tired. It was the end of the school year, and even inside St. George's Episcopal church, it was very hot. Ashamed of my intentions during dinner that August prior, I'd avoided Enid for the ten months since Caroline and I had gotten back together.

"I'd like to talk to you today about the ingredients for happiness," Enid said. She paused. Students and parents leaned in to listen. Usually these speeches were about the eighth-grade class: The nine years the teacher had watched them grow. How we can all remember Sarah when she got stung by that bee! And Rachel when she ate everyone's crackers! And look at them now! Now is the moment for them to go out in the world and put down roots and blossom!

But instead: "People think they know what makes them happy," Enid said. "People think happiness should be permanent. They get upset when it's taken from them. And when they get upset, they complain."

I knew Enid well in some ways. But I had no idea where she was going with this.

"There's so much complaining," Enid said. "I hear it from every one of you students. You complain about grades, about friends, teachers, parents. You complain about the high-school admissions process, the need to leave your friends to go to different institutions. You complain about the Macarena: How everyone is still doing the Macarena. How it's been stuck in your head for over a year. You complain about how everyone knows how to do the Macarena except you."

This was a funny enough line. People laughed. But Enid didn't pause, and it was hard to hear the next couple of sentences over the laughter.

"Many of you think you've been happy over this past year. Your eighth-grade year. When, for the last time, you've been with friends you met when you were little more than babies. You don't want to leave them. You think happiness comes from community, and you've had a great community at St. George's. Every year, eighth-graders cry during the final few weeks of school because they're scared that they're losing the community they've spent nine years building. The only community they've known.

"They're scared that they're leaving their childhoods, and they don't yet know what will replace it. They're scared their relationships with their parents are changing and that they'll lose touch with friends.

"I'm here to tell you that you are right to be scared. You'll never be your mother's little girl or boy again. You'll fall out of touch with many of the classmates around you. And it's normal to cry. Goodbyes to institutions, individuals, and eras in your life should be difficult.

"But I also have good news to share. I am here to tell you that

St. George's is *not* as good as it gets. For those who are ready to move on and for those who want to cling to what they have, you will find future happiness that is greater than any you've felt in the present or the past. It, too, might not be lasting, so you'll have to savor every moment of it once it comes, but I can promise you that you have not yet been as happy as you will be."

She took a step back. It was a short, odd speech, and I was relieved it was done. Parents began tentatively to clap.

Except she continued through the applause: "Some of you think you are happy now. You're going off to Collegiate to wear blue blazers and attend formal dances with the girls from Brearley. Or you're heading to Brearley to memorize poetry and write in tiny handwriting. But you can't find real happiness in high school any more than you can in middle school. You're still at the practice stage of your life. You don't have to live yet. So experiment with the relationships and institutions that will prepare you for the real world."

Enid was by disposition quiet, but when she got going on a subject, she really got going. She had strange associations and spoke them as though everyone could follow with ease. Watching her like this made me something like envious of my former self. I really liked her. I'd loved her. *Nostalgic* is the word that means "envious of my former self."

"Listen to me: This is how you'll find happiness. You will need two things to be happy, neither of which you have right now.

"One: You will need a family of your own. Loved ones who aren't parents or siblings. Close friends and community are good, but they're not enough. I'm talking about a life partner or a child. Some of you will be lucky enough to have both. You need to leave your childhood home and create a home of your own with at least one other person. Love or an arranged marriage; childbirth or adoption. That's why monasteries and nunneries used to be so popular, I think. They were adult families for single, childless people."

Did she miss me? I wondered. But she wasn't talking about me. Did she miss Jacob's father? Impossible. Maybe she didn't miss anyone.

"Two: You will need a second, private thing that matters to you. It can't be fleeting or whimsical. It can't be gluttonous. It can't be television or video games or drugs or sex or drinking or food or sports fandom or political affiliations. It has to be yours, and even if some other people have a thing that's the same as your thing, it needs to be special to you. It needs to provide you meaning because you care about it sincerely and regardless of what other people think. You shouldn't start looking for this second thing until college or after. It might be a job that feels meaningful. It might be a hobby. It might be religion or charity. In Christianity, we speak in terms of the soul. Mr. Keating"—a thrill scampered up my gastrointestinal tract—"teaches that Aristotle used the word *telos* to describe one's reason for being. But I call it *that other, nonfamilial thing.* That thing you need to add to your family to make your life feel complete, purposeful, and entirely yours.

"I can look you all in the eye and tell you that I am happy. Jacob is my family. And art is my soul, my purpose, my telos. Art is how I assert my humanity. How I scream it into the void. It's why I took this job. Teaching allows me time to make my art and help others make theirs. Art is what makes it worthwhile for me to get up every day."

From the murmurs in the church, it was clear that Enid was starting to lose the majority of her audience. The students stopped rolling their eyes and started getting upset. Why was she yelling at them during their graduation ceremony? I thought about standing, climbing up onto the chancel, and giving her a hug, but that would be demeaning, patronizing. I sat on my hands to calm myself. I took a deep breath: In through the nose for four, feel my belly fill up; out through the mouth for six, feel my lips flutter. She continued, going on about how "you have to make sure to devote your life to something that matters to you. Because nothing other than family inherently matters. It's your responsibility to figure out what matters to you. Family plus one other thing. To the graduating eighth-grade class, I say you had neither of those here at St. George's, but nearly all of you will find both. Find your other thing, and be open to finding your people. New people. Find your sources of happiness and cling to them."

She stopped, eventually.

Mr. Hopkins patted my leg in a friendly way.

"You can relax," he said. "She's okay."

He was a kind man, Harold Hopkins, even if he didn't always know how to show it.

(June 1998, continued)

After the ceremony, I took the opportunity to find Jacob and ask how he was doing.

"Good to see you," I said. "You look good." He did. He had put on a little weight.

"I have to get out of here," he said.

It was bright and beautiful where we stood in the churchyard garden. The graduating boys wore dark suits, and the girls wore white dresses. It was a small joy to watch them hug one another and their parents, pose for photos, laugh at inside jokes for what might be the last time.

"Is your mom okay?" I said. "It's nice that she said she's happy, that you make her happy."

"You haven't really spoken to her for a while, right?" he said. "That's what she says. She says you're avoiding her."

Seventh-graders were assigned to pass hors d'oeuvres and lemonade. I took a glass from one student and a multitiered sandwich of thin crisps and mushrooms from another. Though small, the sandwich was still too big to pop in my mouth in one bite, but my other hand was occupied with lemonade. I couldn't figure out how to eat the mushroom crisp. I could bite the top off, leaving the bottom on my napkin, but that would be unseemly. So I held it like a fool. I sipped my lemonade. Caroline and I had a trip planned for a few days later. I wanted to be free of the small mushroom sandwich and on that plane to St. Martin. "No, I haven't really spoken to her lately," I said. "Just in faculty meetings and between classes."

"Honestly, I don't blame you," Jacob said. "At first she was warm with me after Clara dumped me, but lately she has kind of spun out of control."

"About what?" I said.

"Me and Clara," Jacob said.

I focused for the first time.

"What does anything have to do with Clara?"

"Why do you think she said all that stuff about St. George's and high school not mattering? She's obsessed with me getting over Clara. I think she needs to get over Clara too."

"No. Clara — " I started. But then I stopped.

"After Clara and I broke up, Mom tried to talk to her a few times to make sure everything was okay," Jacob said, "and then she got angry at Clara on my behalf or something, but over the past few months… I don't know. It's like she's obsessed with a need to make Clara not be so important to me anymore. To either of us. She loves — loved — Clara as much as I did, I'm starting to realize. Or at least, she loved the person I was when I was with Clara. Mom sees me feeling down, and I think it reminds her that she's sad too. Which makes me angry, and she's definitely angry. We're both angry, and now all she does is work. I've never seen Mom work so hard. She's constantly building and making, photographing, applying for grants. She's telling me to work too."

"To distract yourself from missing Clara?" I said.

"To make Clara matter less," he said. Jacob looked tired. I'm sure he wanted something more from me, but there was nothing I could give.

"Clara doesn't need to matter less," I said. "You can be sad for a bit. That's okay."

(June 1998, continued)

"I saw you talking to Jacob," Richy said after Jacob wandered away. "How's he doing?"

"I don't know," I said, still trying to make sense of how Enid, who was always so much herself, could be influenced by a teenager.

"I saved Jacob and Enid a whole lot of hassle and heartache," Richy said. "Jacob was going to end up at Dalton, but I took that bullet."

"I'm not sure I follow," I said.

"Jacob not getting into Dalton," he said.

"Wait—Jacob *did* get into Dalton?" I said.

"See, that's why I didn't tell you or Enid," he said.

I was getting angry. He was puffing himself up and becoming performative with me in a way that meant something ugly was coming.

"Blink called me last year," Richy said. Blink Hoffman was the longtime head of school at Dalton. "Blink said he was going to accept Clara, of course, and that he was leaning toward accepting Jacob as well. He wanted to hear my thoughts. Blink told me that though

Jacob's grades were far from perfect, his interview and essays were as good as any he'd seen."

"What did Jacob write about?" I asked.

"Apparently something about not knowing what it meant to fit in. That he wanted to figure out what that meant at Dalton. That Dalton seemed like the best place to jar him loose from his world and introduce him to a new one. Blink said it spoke to a real sense of self. But that's not the point. I told Blink that Jacob's mother was a teacher at St. George's and must have written the essays for him."

"Enid would never," I said.

"Well, yes. You and I know that," he said.

Richy made his eyes sparkle.

"Then why?" I said.

"Jacob would have held Clara back," he said. "She's an extraordinary girl, and she deserves the world. She deserves to attend Dalton and have her life launched from there. It's her job to show the world what we're capable of at St. George's."

"But— " I didn't know where to start.

"Now, get this," Richy said. "It means I have to host New Year's Eve three years in a row. You see, usually, Patty and I host one year out in Southampton and then Blink does the next year at his place in Bridgehampton. We all do the whole thing—champagne, caviar, lobsters. But I think when Blink saw I was against Jacob going to Dalton, he started to really want to accept the boy. We had this conversation back in December, so I told him that Patty and I would host two years in a row—that year, which was our turn anyway, and the next—in exchange for his not taking Jacob. He said no. That wasn't enough. Two in a row wasn't enough. He said that in exchange for his not accepting Jacob, I had to host that year, take his slot this year, and then host next year too! Patty wanted my head. But it was worth it. The few grand it will cost me will save Enid more than that in tuition, even with financial aid, and keep Jacob from being a weight around Clara's ankle. They'll never know what I gave up for them."

"You're a maniac."

"Think of your first relationships," he said. "What you would have sacrificed for them. Everything, right? You would have given up everything. This is about Clara. My protecting Clara. She has too much to lose. For herself, and for St. George's reputation. She's got too much potential. In five, ten years, she'll put St. George's on the map. She will be my legacy, your legacy, and the school's. But first she needs to be separated from anything that might slow her down. She needs to grow, to move forward. Climb every goddamned mountain and bring St. George's Episcopal School along with her."

"You're joking," I said.

"You'll see."

I left Richy to find Jacob, who was leaning against the stone of the church, waiting for his mother so they could walk home together.

"Hey," he said.

I didn't know then what to say to Jacob, nor do I know today what I should have said.

"Call me if you ever need to talk," I said.

He said he would, but he didn't. We didn't speak again for more than a decade.

(2008)

In that intervening decade, I didn't see Jacob, and I saw Clara only once. It was a decade briefly defined by prosperity and then by terrorism and fear. I spent quite a bit of time at Yankee Stadium with Richy. For many years, he and I attended every game during the summer months and most games in Mays, Junes, and Septembers. He had season tickets, paid for by St. George's. At the beginning of that decade, we were both approaching sixty. We were both married without biological children. We had both established lives for ourselves that felt suitable to our ambitions. We appeared on the jumbotron frequently and on the YES Network's telecast occasionally; our height difference and the jackets and ties we wore to the games turned us into a reliable sight gag.

Truth is, I spent nearly all my nonteaching, non-Caroline time with Richy. I'd aged out of the friendship-collecting business. I should have been in my friendship-enjoying stage, luxuriating in the relationships that survived. But the friends I'd made after coming to New York and before meeting Caroline were less friends than men around whom I could get very drunk and not be judged for my behavior. Perhaps because I'd devoted myself so much to teaching and to Caroline, the only friendship I had left to enjoy was with a man whom part of me did then and always would despise.

I hated Richy for separating Jacob and Clara, but I hated him for all sorts of other reasons too. For his unchecked ego, for flouting too many rules (even as I flouted others), for treasuring hollow symbols of status, for preening, and for mistreating women as a young man and then thinking that repentance meant redemption. There was no doubt that I hated him. And I'm sure he despised me for my aloofness, my judgment, my lack of interest in all the trivialities he felt composed a life well spent. I've learned that friendship can survive despising. Friendship can survive disgust and disagreement. And envy—I would have liked to have his salary. It would have been nice to be able to purchase for Caroline the paintings she admired in galleries. Now that I can't leave the apartment and she's sometimes forgetful, it would be wonderful to have an original Egon Schiele or Gustav Klimt on the living-room wall. A rich man can buy something like that.

What a friendship can't survive is a lack of vulnerability, but Richy was vulnerable around me in a way I didn't see him be around anyone else.

Watching a baseball game with someone is like driving in a car together. Conversation comes more easily when you're sitting side by side looking out at the world. Richy and I spoke of the players, our students, telos, contrapasso, and the love we had for our wives. He told me that through connections and wise investments, he had made a lot of money. His cousins had told him to invest in India and Brazil, he said. And his money manager was the very best. I deshelled my way through bags of peanuts. Richy preferred not to touch food with his hands. No sandwiches, burgers, chicken wings. No toast or pastries. We sipped our beers. But Richy also spoke of disappointments. He was never offered a professorship at Columbia's Teachers College or even NYU. He wasn't taken seriously as a leader in his field. St. George's was no Trinity or Horace Mann. His wife, Patty, had frequently mentioned her regret at never having had children. He feared he was not enough for her now that they were so often alone together. The genealogical line of the Richard Kingsley Madisons would end with him.

One Sunday when the Yankees were beating up on Kansas City, Richy told me that he had been homesick as a child at boarding school. It had been difficult for him, as he'd wanted always to be around his mother and father. He told me he'd cried a lot at night, lonely for his parents. He'd concluded that his parents were selfish. They'd spent the remainder of a dwindling fortune on themselves and just enough on his education to make him money-hungry and poor. He lost them both over the course of this decade, and I was with him at both funerals. He talked about how the grief was painful but that he was lucky in his ability to transfer so much of the attachment he'd had for his parents to Patty. That was what home meant to him: one or two people who made him feel safe.

I—who'd hardly known my parents—argued that he was conflating or confusing emotions. With romantic love, there was choice, and that constant choice to reaffirm that love was what made it so powerful. Much more powerful than love between parents and children. Looking back, I realize I was talking nonsense. I recall that conversation now because in this moment, I need to believe Caroline cares for me as a partner and not as a child. I need to believe our love is and could only be romantic. That even in my current state, you are constantly choosing me anew.

The other day Caroline looked at me as though confused. It scared me. I was in my chair and she was in the kitchen making eggs. Henry had visited the previous day but was able to stay for only an hour. Caroline didn't like the caregivers from the service lingering beyond the time necessary to clean my equipment. Now she turned to me and saw me with my nasal cannula and my IV. It had been a rough week, and I was happy for all the extra oxygen and nutrients I could get. She saw me and for a moment she looked terrified by what was on and around me, like she'd forgotten what state I was in. But then she righted herself. Reconciled herself to the present. And to the future as well. She was back. And she chose to love me again.

From 2001 to 2007, the Yankees won over ninety games every season, made it to the playoffs every year, and didn't win a single World Series. That sums up rather well how I felt about my life too. Things were good. Very good. I had nothing to complain about. Maybe there wasn't the ecstasy of a championship, but I was confident and still at close to the top of my game. There was hope every year.

That said, it was painful to watch Jeter, Mariano, and Posada—as good as they still were—age into less dynamic versions of their younger selves. And Teixeira and Swisher were cheeseballs. Too quick with the dopey canned smiles. But A-Rod joined the team in 2003 or so, and as much as I wanted to dislike him, his swing was the most beautiful I'd ever seen. Leg up, bat tipped back like Mickey Mantle's, front elbow pulled in, hands close to his shoulder, barrel dropped, and then once he was on plane, his hands came forward and through the baseball in an explosion of torque that combined shot put with ballet. Winning or losing had nothing to do with it.

(November 1998)

The one time I did see Clara in that decade after she graduated from St. George's was in her sophomore year of high school. She called St. George's and left a message inviting me to an event. She said I could bring Mr. Madison if I wanted to, and as much as I didn't want to, it seemed wrong not to pass along the invite. The purpose of the get-together and when exactly it occurred are both hazy to me, but it had something to do with celebrating Dalton's scholarship students. The language dripped with euphemism. It was a night to honor "Students of Diverse Backgrounds" or it was an afternoon to acknowledge "Dalton's Ring of Support."

But in practice, it was a gathering of the students on financial aid and their families. Blink Hoffman held it in the Dalton gymnasium, where white folding tables were covered in plastic Dalton Tigers tablecloths. I thought the invitation might be Clara's way of paying me back for teaching her, covering for her, and setting her on a right path. I was touched.

When I arrived, Clara was seated with a boy who was dressed

conservatively. He wore glasses and a V-neck sweater. Their posture together seemed affectionate, and I was relieved that Clara had friends. But Clara was awkward in shaking my hand. She didn't stand up when I arrived. Maybe she was embarrassed, or maybe she regretted attending at all.

It was unnerving to see Clara in real life after spending fifteen months thinking about her in the abstract. Jacob and Richy talked about her explicitly, Enid obliquely, and I'd already made her a legend when I introduced the Ember Exam to the two eighth-grade classes following hers. But here she was in person. More awkward than I remembered her. She couldn't, or didn't want to, meet my eyes.

Clara introduced her friend to me as Aaron. After standing and shaking my hand, Aaron left us, and I asked Clara if Dalton suited her and if she'd spoken to Jacob. She answered monosyllabically: Yes. No. There was too much noise.

"I need to ask you something!" she shouted.

"Anything!" I shouted.

Then she lowered her voice and spoke, and I couldn't hear what she said.

Most of the other fifty-odd students in the room were surrounded by families with whom they seemed comfortable. Their comfort emphasized the discomfort between me and Clara. All the families seemed to know one another, and though many went out of their way to introduce themselves to us, no one joined our table, which was set for ten. Caterers served sushi and passed around lemon water and white wine. It was all very tasteful and uncomfortable.

I drank four glasses of white wine. Clara and I looked at the banners from the years Dalton had won various boys' and girls' volleyball and basketball tournaments.

"I don't know how to say it!" she shouted, or she shouted something like that.

"What?" I said, which could have been taken to mean either "To say what?" or "What? I can't hear you."

She said something and smiled. I smiled and nodded.

I drank another glass of white wine before Richy arrived, hugged us both, ran up to shake Blink Hoffman's hand, and ran back saying, "Dalton! Look at us here at Dalton!" Richy shook hands with the parents and uncles and aunts of other students. He piled sushi onto his plate and shouted to Clara, "Tell us! Tell us everything! I can't tell you how excited I was when Mr. Keating passed along your invitation."

"I'm fine," she shouted. She looked distracted. "I haven't really been in touch with anyone from St. George's."

"Good for you!" Richy shouted. She had his full attention. "Academics?" he shouted.

"I did well on a math test last year," she shouted. "An important math test."

"Of course you did!" Richy shouted. "Starting last year, Mr. Keating and I got season tickets to the Yankees!"

"Yeah?" she shouted.

"We go to nearly all the games, and we were just talking about you, wondering how you were doing, so when Mrs. Cooper told Mr. Keating you'd called to invite us to this event, I can't tell you how happy you made us back at old St. George's! I called up Blink to check in on you, and he affirmed that you were the real deal. He's got high hopes for you too!"

Clara looked distracted and embarrassed again. She and Richy yelled to each other about whether the Yankees could rely on the current starting rotation. The music was very loud, or maybe it was because of the acoustics of the basketball courts that I had trouble hearing, but either way, while other families were milling about, she or Richy thought the Yankee pitching staff was the best in the AL East, and she or Richy thought it wasn't to be trusted. I was sweating. I wanted to leave, and I was about to invent an excuse, but then the music stopped and Blink Hoffman was tapping the mic.

Blink was a pasty, green-hued man. We'd met a few times before and I always needed to reintroduce myself. Blink wore the same jackets and ties as Richy but sloppily. His very expensive clothing was too big for his big goofy body. He looked like he lived on Wild Turkey and whole milk. He was tall and thin except for a large gut, and instead of belting his pants above or below his stomach, he cinched his buckle right where he was largest. I'd never seen a man belt his pants like that before. He was always yanking his belt from one side to the other, but never up or down. I like to think it was his way of telling the world to fuck off.

"I'm so excited to have such an illustrious group of young people here with your families to celebrate your presence at Dalton," he said. He had the squeaky voice of a young boy, and he cleared his throat often as he spoke. He yanked his belt to one side. "The fact that you, hmm, as a group, don't each individually have the thirty thousand dollars a year to attend Dalton and that you found your way here anyway indicates that no matter what you might be enduring at the moment, you truly represent the best of the best.

"You are the Dalton Way personified. I have faith that even if the fathers here—I see you laughing—don't own the biggest commercial real estate firms in the country, you have raised your kids, the kids here with us, these young Dalton men and women, to be special. They might build the biggest commercial real estate firms in the country. They—you, students, I'm talking to you—might, no, *must* write the great American novel. You might teach the world to see itself in some entirely new way."

Everyone applauded. What else could they do.

"So I've gathered you, Dalton's best, the future America's brightest, a small group but a group of MVPs—that's 'most valuable players' for some of the moms out there—" And here folks laughed. "Or in our case, should I say most valuable pupils?" Everyone laughed again.

The wine had been flowing for a long time, and the crowd was in a generous spirit. Only the students looked appalled. But high-school students always look appalled. Everything to them is awkward or false. It's why I prefer to teach eighth-graders.

Blink Hoffman yanked his belt to the other side. He said, "So, as I was saying, I've gathered all my MVPs—our most valuable pupils, the best of the best, or, if not yet, at least those who will become the best of the best—to meet the best of all time. Ladies and gentlemen, may I introduce you to a Dalton special, hmm, may I introduce you to the MVP of two World Series, the best pitcher in the history of Major League Baseball, Sandy Koufax!"

Of the fifty students in attendance, maybe one or two had heard of Sandy Koufax. Even Clara, a baseball fan, was not impressed. But I was. Mr. Koufax held himself upright but relaxed. He was a rosy-cheeked, gray-haired slim old man in khakis and a blue-and-white-checkered button-down, but I don't think another celebrity existed who could get Richy and me so excited.

Sandy Koufax! The youngest player ever to be inducted into the Hall of Fame. What he said that afternoon at Dalton wasn't memorable, but we applauded loudly.

Afterward, Richy, still spry in his fifties, ran up to see the great man. He waited in line, and when it was his turn to shake hands, Richy made him laugh. They talked until those behind Richy gave up and wandered away. Richy and Sandy exchanged business cards. Sandy slapped Richy on the back. With this second occasion to talk to Clara without Richy there, I looked around for her, intending to ask what it was she'd wanted to discuss. But Clara had left without saying goodbye.

What Richy had said in the spring—that Clara would be our legacy—stuck with me. I'd never put much stock in the concept of legacy. It seemed the coin of a more aristocratic realm. Or of politicians and professional athletes. Al Gore and Derek Jeter had legacies to worry about. Not me. But then again, I didn't have kids of my own. I had Caroline. And Henry. They were my family. I had another thing too. Teaching. The Ember Exam. My students. And of all my students, there was Clara. It had been less than two years since I'd taught her, but I'd waited twenty years for her, and I already understood there'd never be another one. I had taught Clara, enabled her life in some small way, and my future would in part be defined by her accomplishments and limitations.

(March 2002)

That's not to say that after Clara graduated, I stopped caring. In fact, she'd helped me see the potential of what I was doing come to fruition, and I taught with more gusto than ever. Though Clara might have been unique, I could nonetheless make sure that twenty more years of students would benefit from whatever it was I had to give. I analyzed my strengths and deficits. Eliminated obstacles to student learning. Inaugurated the Ember Land Fair.

Twenty tables, fifty poster boards, fifty eighth-graders in the fluorescent-lit gymnasium. Kai Cooper paced back and forth, reciting softly. Kai might not have been Clara, but he was important to me in his way. I taught for him as I taught for all of them.

The Ember Land Fair looked just like Szilvia's science fair, but my students had no scientific method. Their only job was to *affect the audience.* It was now 8:00 a.m., and by 9:50, parents, teachers, fifth-, sixth-, and seventh-graders would start cycling through. My eighth-graders' goal was to change these visitors' vision of the world. That had been my only instruction. It would be my only criterion for grading. The more Harold Hopkins demanded I produce a rubric, the more I found the concept contemptible.

"Where's your rubric!" Mr. Hopkins had shouted in the faculty lounge the day before.

"The kids have to create a lasting literary memory!" I shouted back. "How's that for a rubric!"

They could write or just recite a poem, but that meant memorization and planting their feet on the gymnasium floor and making the listener *feel.* They could explain a grammatical rule, which meant that each visitor had to leave the fair with a new understanding of the English language. Students could write a character study, but the person described — uncle, celebrity, stranger on the 6 train — needed to be alive on the page. Needed to live. Emotion, knowledge, entertainment: It all counted. Every student had to be remembered for something good.

School uniforms were white and khaki and powder blue. A few boys, like Kai, wore sports coats. That morning, Enid wore a peasant dress with pockets in the front. She was better at fixing poster-board mishaps than I was. Caroline and I were happy together, and Enid had rediscovered her equanimity. I'd missed Enid and was glad to be her friend again. I wore a three-piece tweed suit, heavy enough that I hadn't needed an overcoat on the way to school, but now I was sweating. The first visitors, fifth-graders, would charge in at any moment.

"I hate to agree with Harold," Enid said as we watched the eighth-graders bounce and squirm. It was too early in the morning, and I'd given them each a jelly doughnut on the way in. Caroline had made jelly doughnuts. Boys covered in powdered sugar arm-wrestled on the floor. Then they just straight-up wrestled. Girls bent to break them up and were dragged down too. Girls fought back, hugged, or shrieked. Uniforms were creased and rumpled. Enid and I ignored them. There was joy in being bad guardians. In being bad. "I hate to agree with Harold, but you should have been more specific," Enid said. "Some of these kids wrote novels and others just memorized a poem?"

"Not novels," I said. "Character studies, and that's the point! I love Szilvia to death but her science fair is too paint-by-numbers. 'Look at this geranium that died because I kept it in the closet!'" I imitated past students. "'And look at this geranium that survived in just a little light! And look at this geranium with lots of light that thrived!'"

"All right, all — " Enid said, pretending not to enjoy my routine.

"'Check out this baby tooth after two weeks in Coca-Cola!'" I said. "'It's all black! Now check out this one after two weeks in orange juice! Dark brown! And in water? No change at all!'"

"Stop it," she said. "I get that you're anxious, but calm down." Boys and girls rolled around in one big pile. Only Kai was off to the side, by the padded gym walls. "And you stop it," Enid scolded the students. "Get back to your stations. The fifth-graders are almost here. Tuck in your shirts!"

They scattered to their poster boards and groomed themselves. Enid stood beside me. I looked at her. I'd known her for thirty years. We had been in love for a few of those. She wasn't my person, but she was a person who had been mine for a time, and I loved her still. I'd gotten old, and she'd gotten old, and there I was in the gymnasium with an affection for her that I didn't know what to do with. I thanked her for her help.

* * *

Enid told Kai he should always button a jacket's middle button, sometimes the top one, but never the bottom one. At first he seemed not to believe her, but she was firm with him. Dusted off his shoulders. Fixed his tie. She crossed the gym back to me. "He'll be all right. He said he's never done anything like this before." I nodded. "Tara told me her plan was to 'definitively explain the difference between *whomever* and *whoever*.' She used the word *definitively*! Is that your word or hers?"

"All her," I said.

"She said she wanted her classmates to think about her from now on whenever they used *whomever*. It's adorable."

The kids were passing around several monstrous Starbucks drinks of milk, syrups, and whipped cream they regularly picked up on the way to school.

"I wish you'd done this for Jacob," she said.

"I know," I said. "Me too."

"It's spring break," she said. "For college kids. Jacob's home."

"Has he declared a major?" I said.

"On Saturday night, I locked up like I always do, but when I was brushing and flossing, I heard him open the dead bolt. He's on his own now. He can go out at night if he wants to, and I don't bother with a curfew, but I was having trouble sleeping. Later on, I heard the door creak open, so I peeked out and saw Clara heading into his room."

"You sure it was her?" I said.

"I asked him about it the next day," she said.

A poster board fell and was righted. The fifth-grade teachers opened the gymnasium door.

"Did he come clean?" I said.

"It wasn't that," she said. "He just said that sometimes Clara comes down and sleeps in his bed. He said there was nothing going on between them. She just sleeps there sometimes. He said it used to happen in high school too."

The fifth-graders were swarming. My eighth-graders weren't prepared for them. How could they be? Fifth-graders are like first-graders. They do what they're told. But also, they slide around on their knees on the polished gymnasium floor. They were scared of the eighth-graders. They wanted to look cool. They thought sliding on their knees made them look cool. They wanted to learn. They wanted to be seen by their teachers to be learning. It's hard to be ten, just like it's hard to be thirteen and it's hard to be seventy-five.

A curt word from one of their teachers, and the fifth-graders scattered with pre-appointed buddies to listen to poems and grammar rules. The eighth-graders braced themselves. Some became artists and most became teachers. Such is the way of the world.

Kai was about to begin. A dozen kids surrounded him. Kai was tall for an eighth-grader. A giant compared to the fifth-graders. He had a broken-nose handsomeness. His sports coat fit him well. Kai Cooper. Not the best student, but he cared. He was shaking, standing up in front of the fifth-graders. Some eighth-graders left their posts to come watch too.

I was at his side.

"I can't do this, Mr. Keating," he said. "I don't want to do this."

"You have to," I said.

The ceiling on my teaching hadn't been the material. I knew the material; after years of tinkering I'd gotten the Ember Exam to where I wanted it. We read *Romeo and Juliet* and *The Razor's Edge*. The ceiling on my teaching had been my lack of insight into each student. I'd been relying on instinct and guesswork. That had to stop. I needed to know every single one of them better. For the class after Jacob and Clara's, I had each student sit for entry interviews. An hour conversation with each. But the students just told me what they thought I wanted to hear. So I spent the following summer creating a series of diagnostic assessments. I asked questions about their home life. I asked about grammar, art, and how their brains worked. But they didn't know how to respond.

The summer before the first Ember Land Fair, I discovered the Enneagram and Myers-Briggs. Pseudoscience, maybe, but more useful than anything I'd invented. Kai was an Enneagram 4 and an INFP. Accordingly, he needed something, wanted to create something and share it with others. But still, I was just guessing.

"I wouldn't make you do this if I didn't know you could," I said.

And, of course, he did it. I don't remember his specific words but the poem described a playground near his house when he'd been younger. He was playing on the swings, and a group of boys scared his father. The poem was about him and his need to protect his father. It was in iambic hexameter. His feeling that his father wanted to be able to protect him. His father walked with a cane and was ashamed of it. But Kai wasn't ashamed of his father. Kai had cried in real life as a younger kid and he cried again now as an eighth-grader in the gymnasium when the poem was finished. The fifth-graders cheered. So did Kai's classmates. They all went crazy. *Again!* they chanted. *Again! Again! Again!*

(March 2019)

Growing up, I heard more than a few times the following joke: "Your mama is so fat, when she sits around the house, she *really* sits around the house."

The joke relies on the double meaning of *sitting around*. In the first sense, your mama *sitting around* the house just means your mama hangs out in her house, a perfectly normal thing for your mama to do. In the second case, her *sitting around* means physically surrounding the house — being so fat that somehow her body subsumes the house.

The problem is that bodies — even enormous ones — can't physically sit around houses. Your mama could sit *on* a house or she could have her body stick out of house windows, but *around* doesn't really work here. Grammatically, the joke fails.

But it also fails on the level of humanity: Why is it acceptable to mock those whose bodies have gotten out of their control? Why attempt to hurt someone by making him think his mother is repulsive? Because that's the point, isn't it? Jokes like this one rely on forcing the recipient to think about his mother as an object of contempt. And my mother wasn't terrible. But neither was she available to me. So I think about these jokes. I'd have liked to have any mother, fat or thin. Obese, emaciated. Even a mother confined forever to a wheelchair. I return to these jokes these days in a way I know is not healthy. But I'm not in control of where my mind goes.

I heard this specific sit-around-the-house joke enough times over the years that I looked into it and was interested to find that it originally mocked the bowlegged. Before modern medicine discovered the importance of vitamin D, being bowlegged was a relatively common, visible, and embarrassing affliction, not unlike being obese today.

It was Henny Youngman who seems to have originated the joke. In the early 1950s, during an appearance on the TV program *This Is Show Business,* he said, "I don't say my wife is bowlegged, but when she sits around the house, she sits around the house." Which makes sense! Bowlegged people's legs bend in extreme ways, so sitting *around* a house would make the joke work.

My guess is that the musicality of "when she sits around the house, she sits around the house" was just too good to give up, so once folks stopped being bowlegged, fat was the best replacement.

As you can tell from most of the jokes in this novel, I'm not one for insults. I don't find it funny to be overweight. A person is a person is a person. A mother is a mother is a mother.

But now that I can't move my ever-shrinking body, I admit to finding myself somewhat resentful of those persons I used to pity. The overweight, the asymmetrical, the very short, the acned, the recipients of bad haircuts, the newly fired or laid off, the recently discarded, the poor and hungry—what I wouldn't do to trade places with any of them for a single day. I'd give a year of my life for a day of theirs. I'd give a decade for a week. In that day or week, I would gorge myself on the sweetest foods. I would hug my loved ones. I would tell Caroline everything she means to me and go to bed with her a thousand times. If necessary, I would steal. What could they do? Put me in jail? When I'm already imprisoned in this body? I don't know what I would do, but I would seize that day, that week. I pity no one anymore. My condition has made me a worse person, I think, as I run through the most memorable mama jokes:

1. *Your mama is so fat, her cereal bowl comes with a lifeguard!*
2. *Your mama is so fat, the sign outside one restaurant says* Maximum occupancy 512 — or your mama!
3. *Your mama is so fat, she was born with a silver shovel in her mouth!*
4. *Your mama is so fat, she's on both sides of the family!*
5. *Your mama is so fat, when she fell over, she rocked herself asleep trying to get up again.*
6. *Your mama is so fat, she fell in love and broke it.*
7. *Your mama is so fat, when she was diagnosed with a flesh-eating disease, the doctor gave her ten* years *to live!*

All these jokes make perfect sense, though only one is funny. Care to play a game? Return to the list now and see if you can spot the funny one.

Okay.

Are you ready?

Part III

Clara the Elder

(February 2006)

I referenced Christophe Lejeune toward the beginning of the book. He was a cofounder of Bananalytics, a company you would have heard of if I called it by its similarly ludicrous real name. My stepson, Henry, is an inventor. He worked with Monsieur Lejeune years ago and subsequently invited him to celebratory events. Six or seven years after that evening with Clara at Dalton, Monsieur Lejeune and I met at a party held in honor of Henry after Walmart put in an order for a hundred thousand units of the Mamaroo, an ingenious contraption Henry invented that rocks a baby back and forth in just the right way when parents are tired of doing so themselves.

Monsieur Lejeune was obese, but in a different way than Blink Hoffman. Monsieur Lejeune was round like a sphere, whereas Blink looked pregnant like a lady. Dressed in layers, never fidgeting, Lejeune was fully at ease with himself, though his obesity was unusual among those who made their careers in tech. (I find myself body-obsessed now that I have lost the use of my own. Muscularity doesn't seem right for either

Blink or Christophe. Neither can be made small, as Richy can, so I make Blink and Christophe large. I envy their aching knees and the moments in the shower when they wish they were young again.) I asked Christophe how he'd found life in Silicon Valley, and he said that he'd always enjoyed it there. He said that as an obese man, he was memorable. His comfort with the word, like his obesity itself, made him stand apart. All those clean-cut thin men with their start-ups and starched jeans, dress shirts, short haircuts, and blue blazers. They were all the same man, he said. They all went to Stanford undergrad or Wharton grad or they'd dropped out of Harvard or Carnegie Mellon. But not Monsieur Lejeune. He was just an obese French kid who graduated from Minnesota State and loved to eat and read and make people laugh.

I was no one to Monsieur Lejeune but he never let his eyes wander when we spoke at that first party. It turned out that, like many Frenchmen, he was a great reader of twentieth-century American fiction, and though we disagreed with each other on nearly everything, what a pleasure it was to find someone to disagree with about Paul Auster at a party celebrating a large order of Mamaroos.

The next time Monsieur Lejeune and I met was at another party to honor Henry, this time for starting a new company that had invented the world's best toddler cage, something he called the Breeze play yard. Monsieur Lejeune had by that point gathered some more information about me, and when he saw me at the restaurant, he looked excited. He asked me if, in my teaching, I'd ever crossed paths with—and he went on to list a few names I didn't recognize before ending with Clara's.

"You know *Clara*!" I said.

"*You* know Clara!" he said.

Our mutual knowing of Clara created a fellow feeling that drew us together and to a corner where we could trade stories. Clara would have been in her early twenties then. He asked what she had been like as a girl. I asked what she was like as an adult. I had more to say than he did and he was interested in all of it, but finally he told his story:

Monsieur Lejeune had worked in Silicon Valley for the past fifteen years as a kind of jolly general consultant or floating chief strategic officer. He'd been there since his externship at Minnesota State, which required every student to take a year off in the middle of their education and join the workforce. Most worked on Wall Street or in hockey journalism or whatever else you're imagining a twenty-year-old at Minnesota State might find enticing, but Monsieur Lejeune made photocopies for a company designing microchips outside San Francisco. He didn't know anything about microchips and never learned anything about them, but after he got his bachelor's degree, he went back and bounced around, buying small percentages of companies that eventually failed or were sold. From the ones that were sold, he was able to put away a few hundred thousand dollars, which was more than he'd ever imagined possible. During this time, he became fixated on what might be done with all the data that was out there.

The sheer volume of unsorted information — people's locations and purchasing preferences, where thirty- to thirty-five-year-old Angelenos walked their dogs in the morning, where suburban Detroiters bought their coffee, who preferred gel to mousse, what brand of gel people who bought their coffee pre-ground liked to use, what kind of men women dated if those women had grad-school degrees or just college or just high school, which restaurants, flights, basketball camps, wedding rings, people liked. There was so much out there to collect, to collate, to use to figure out what anyone might do next. Or, more important, what they might buy next.

Lejeune found himself growing obsessed, data points swirling like disco lights in his mind, and amid the product managers and engineers and graphic designers at the tech-bro parties he frequented, he managed to find a few like-minded folks, a few fellow obsessives eager to make sense of all this information and then process and sell it. This small group — which included the CEO of a new breast-pump company, an MIT-trained physicist who played guitar in a successful jam band, and an LSAT tutor — began meeting every Tuesday to discuss analytics over cheap Mexican food and banana sodas.

One day, a young woman came in with the MIT guitarist. She had bright blue eyes and short hair, and she was wearing a turquoise velour jumpsuit.

Lejeune told me he'd never seen anything like her. At first, he assumed she was the actress girlfriend of the wannabe rock star, but as soon as she sat down with them, he saw she was something else entirely. She talked fast, lecturing, and "kept up with me taco for taco." He thought she must be coked up. But she knew more — had thought more — about analytics than he had. She was so exactly what he was looking for at that moment "that it almost seemed I had invented her."

She kept coming on Tuesday evenings, and after a while he realized she wasn't coked up at all, just somewhat unmoored. She was working for another French guy, an asshole who was trying to start a company that sold wine online.

Unlike every other one of his countrymen he'd met in the States,

Christophe loved America and tried to become more American, or at least more San Franciscan, which to him was an important distinction. He hated folks like Clara's boss and maybe boyfriend who seemed to come to America just to stand out as exceptionally French. Part of Christophe wanted to save Clara from the other French guy. "To be frank," he admitted, he also saw in her someone who could move his career forward. It was unclear to me whether Clara was dating the MIT guitarist, her boss, both, or neither, but I didn't want to interrupt to ask superfluous questions.

Christophe liked Clara as a friend. He admitted he had a crush on her, but he also wanted her to be his business partner. And as that latter instinct was the one he trusted more, they tended to talk shop. He let her choose the other members of the Tuesday-night group she trusted, and they started Bananalytics. The four of them — Christophe, Clara, the MIT guitarist, and the breast-pump guy. The guitarist agreed to quit his band before the year was up. The breast-pump guy was in talks to sell his share of the business to his partner. Clara griped about working for the French guy; griped about dating him too.

So the four of them kept up their Tuesday meetings, building out a business plan for purchasing, collecting, and repackaging data to sell on the open market. Once in a while, when Clara needed an escape, she and Christophe met for a drink. For a few months, even though she was some seven or eight years younger than he was, she was his closest friend. They talked about Edward Lorenz's missteps in chaos theory. They talked about the need for a Democratic Congress to rein in George W. Bush. She told him about Dalton kids' chauffeurs and chefs, and the history of judo. "She talked about her family and going to a small school in downtown Manhattan, which was why I bothered mentioning her name to you to begin with."

It was at this point that Monsieur Lejeune told me the story about when Clara was young and her family didn't eat for a couple days because her mother was too sick and her father too agoraphobic to go outside. I listened with horror, having had no idea Clara had ever been in such need. *What kind of teacher am I to let something like that go on?* I thought, though the answer was that I was a teacher like 99 percent of other teachers. I'd taught her for nine months, years after those events occurred, and she was one of fifty students I was teaching at that time. Yes, she was a special case, due not only to her academic excellence but also to her relationship with Jacob. But I wasn't an at-home interventionist. My job was to introduce eighth-graders to topic sentences and quotation analysis. I fear I protest too much. Anyway, it was the end of Monsieur Lejeune's story that interested me most:

"So we banana-soda drinkers arranged to meet—just the four of us—at a shmancy hotel bar to plan our final move. We were all going to officially quit our jobs the following week, and the idea was to build courage and toast the formation of the first pure data-analytics company in the internet age. I don't think I'd ever been more optimistic about anything, and, as I see you're somewhat familiar with the Bananalytics story, I'm sure you have some sense that our optimism wasn't entirely misplaced.

"But Clara texted the day before to tell us she had a different plan. 'A larger ambition,' I think she wrote. She was, what, twenty-three, twenty-four, we were in our thirties, and our plan to harvest all the data in the world wasn't big enough for her! She didn't return our calls. I haven't heard from her since."

(June 2006)

"I had to share the news with you the moment I hung up," Richy said.

"I'm supposed to be supervising them while they clean out their lockers," I said.

Another class of eighth-graders was about to graduate. It was an indistinct class, full of kindhearted, unmemorable students. I taught for so many years, only the outliers stick in my memory. The unusually gifted, funny, sad, or cruel. This group was fine. Nice enough. Perfectly industrious. They were sure to move on to high school, college, then law school or investment banking. Interior design. Commercial real estate. They'd have jobs and babies, and their babies would have babies and elect presidents and die or invent medical interventions to let them live forever.

"Lockers?" Richy said. "Lockers always end up cleared. There's no time for lockers. Sit down."

I reclined in the Eames chair across from his Chippendale desk. The Satsuma vase had its own table in the corner.

"I just heard the most wonderful news about Clara," he said.

I sat up straighter.

"Well, I can't claim to understand it all, but I hear from my cousin's guy out west that Clara is on fire in San Francisco. She's already made a name for herself. She was working with some guys on understanding data — "

"I know," I said. "Analytics. I was the one who told you about that."

"Will you listen?" he said. "But instead of the data play, she and her partner focused all their attention on a single product — some kind of bracelet that will change the way we live."

"How would a — " I started. I was trying to make sense of the timeline between what Christophe had told me four months earlier and what I was hearing now. Her partner must be the French guy Christophe hated. The bracelet must be what she'd abandoned Christophe in order to build.

"All I know," he said, "is that Clara was working for this guy who had a prototype, but Clara was the one who realized its potential. People around San Francisco are wearing them already. My cousin is on the waiting list, and they're turning away investors. My cousin actually called me because I'd been talking about Clara for years, and when he realized my Clara was the same Clara he'd been hearing about, he couldn't believe it.

"But I knew it!" Richy cried triumphantly. "Hoo-yah! I knew that if we took that girl — our girl — and pointed her in the right direction, she would change the world, and just a couple years out of college she's already doing it.

"Forget about her potential to donate to the school. I'm not just talking about the money she can give. Forget about her commencement speeches and new classrooms named for her. She'll be the reason New York's heaviest hitters start touring St. George's.

"'This is the classroom where Clara Hightower learned algebra. Allow me to introduce you to the teacher who taught her to read. We were where it all happened. Where Clara Hightower came from. Her family didn't have the ambition. Dalton just iced the cake. It was St. George's Episcopal School in downtown Manhattan, New York City, that boosted Clara into orbit!'"

"I'm going to go make sure those lockers get cleaned," I said.

(June 2006, continued)

I called Enid that evening. She'd already heard the news. She'd spoken to Clara a month or two back.

"And you didn't think to mention it?" I said.

"You don't tell me every time you speak to a former student," she said.

"You know I care for Clara," I said.

"Get in line," she said.

"So what's with the bracelet?" I said. "Sounds exciting."

"Sounds pretty silly to me. A bracelet that makes all your decisions for you?"

"I'm not sure I understand," I said.

"I'm not sure anyone does," she said. "Clara asked me if I wanted to try one. They're in beta testing, she says. They've made a few thousand of these things. It's supposed to be an alarm clock, and it tells you what to eat—or when to eat? And you can check in at places? Like, it tells your friends where you've been?"

"Forget the tech," I said. "How is she doing? How did she sound?"

“We spoke for only five minutes,” Enid said. “I call her a few times a year, and she never picks up, but this time she did. I didn’t want to hurt her feelings when she asked if I wanted a bracelet, but it seemed such a waste to send one to me. I already know when to wake up and when to eat. Clara is so much better than these people.”

(May 2019)

The past couple of weeks have been difficult. I've been unable to write. I couldn't think clearly. Clara wasn't on my mind. Just mist and clouds and the body that can't feel except weight or ache or something in between. Doctors are useless. They smile at me and talk to Caroline. I don't blame them. What are they supposed to do?

I've chosen to tell Clara's story because I don't know how I'd explain my own. How to explain my particular variety of pain that is the same as fatigue and itch and loneliness, because even if I tried to explain it to Caroline, who is living it alongside me, I'd need metaphor. No one who hasn't been stuck inside a nonfunctional body can imagine what it's like. How awful it is when no one visits, and how awful it is when someone does. It's like what a fish feels when the water around him suddenly freezes. It's like what a baby feels when it leaves the womb, except it's the opposite of that, except there is no opposite of that. It's probably something like watching your child die. I'm getting farther away, not closer. My body itches and I can't scratch. My limbs are sore and I can't stretch them. Blades are forever slicing off the skin of my fingers and toes. I'm hungry but I can't eat. My eyes are dry. I am hot, stiff, aching, itching, bored, constipated. I am heavy, full, angry. My God, am I angry.

But these are just words.

Clara is the closest I've come to greatness. Clara is my legacy, even if she also belongs to countless others. So I tell jokes and try to make Clara come alive. I try to provide wishes fulfilled. Clara's. Yours. My own.

WIRED PROFILES FEB 18, 2007 1:30 P.M.

CAN'T CATCH CLARA

Clara Hightower grew up in a cramped inner-city apartment, and now the boys of Silicon Valley are running behind her trying to catch up. Could her Everything Bracelet be the secret to good health?

You've seen them around San Francisco. The first few times, you probably didn't know what you were looking at. Or maybe a friend called you in disbelief screaming that she finally got one! And it works! She's never slept better in her life. Or she's finally eating healthy again.

I hadn't heard of the Everything Bracelet six months ago. And now, on the cusp of Everything Inc. completing its Series B at a valuation of over $50 million, they suddenly seem to be everywhere; one morning I saw them on six different wrists as I waited for my coffee at the Starbucks at the corner of Union and Laguna.

Two years ago, when Jean-Michel Husson presented Hightower with a prototype — a flat thin band with its now-signature gunmetal finish — she liked the look but didn't understand why Husson would limit the bracelet to its check-in function. Husson had originally conceived the gadget as a way to tap in and out of restaurants, cafés, and bars, receive discounts, and connect to a database where your friends could find you if you weren't picking up your phone. But Hightower saw far more potential. She wanted it to be the Swiss Army knife of technology. And now in some circles that gunmetal band is as iconic as the Swiss Army knife's glossy red casing.

Though Hightower spurns publicity — she made the unusual decision not to be interviewed or photographed for this profile — Husson, her business and romantic partner, was more than happy to give her the credit. "All these ideas are floating around in SF, and for the first time in human history, because of the internet, we have the data. That was what Clara saw so clearly. We know about REM sleep cycles, we know about different kinds of caloric intake for men and women, and we know about how heartbeat and body temperature relate to sleep and eating. So though she loved my original vision, she kept saying, 'More, more, more — we must add more.'"

You might be wondering how much more. It's a fashion accessory. It lets your friends access your whereabouts. Based on pulse-measurement technology and user-entered timing preferences, it wakes you up at the optimal time for your body. It tells you when you're hungry versus when you just want the sensation of eating. And this is just the beginning.

"At the moment, it's primarily a health tool," Husson explained. "If you want to lose weight, it will help you. If you want to get more and better sleep, it will help you. If you want to relax knowing your friends are able to find you, it can do that too. In the future, it might, for example, let you know more about the optimal times to try to make a baby! Clara has a list of a hundred more potential functionalities."

Is this too much for one tool? Richard Kingsley Madison IV, an early mentor of Hightower's, doesn't think so. "Clara can do anything," Madison told me. "Her whole life, people have always been trying to keep up, to catch Clara. But they never could." He added that he is not surprised she's sitting on the hottest product in San Francisco with a wait list of potential investors as long as that of those eager to get their hands on the hardware. "Some people compare her to Steve Jobs," Madison says, "others to Thomas Edison or Henry Ford. But Clara has been a rocket ship ever since she was a little girl at St. George's Episcopal School in downtown Manhattan. Though she comes from nothing — she lived in the most difficult circumstances, much worse than any other St. George's student — she had the intelligence, the ambition, and the genius for . . . well, for anything she focused on. A rocket ship. All we needed to do was point her in the right direction! Now that she's blasted off, who knows where she'll land?"

(May 2019, continued)

The purpose of an extended metaphor is to communicate the essence of a thing by comparing it to something else.

My personal favorite is from *Gatsby,* when Nick Carraway compares the desolate land between Manhattan and Long Island to a valley of ashes: “This is a valley of ashes — a fantastic farm where ashes grow like wheat into ridges and hills and grotesque gardens; where ashes take the forms of houses and chimneys and rising smoke and, finally, with a transcendent effort, of men who move dimly and already crumbling through the powdery air.”

At first, the reader imagines the land as not only ugly and polluted but also burned and destroyed.

Good start. And he uses the jalapeño principle: *Ashes, chimneys, smoke, crumbling,* and *powdery* all force the reader to think of burning and decay.

But then Fitzgerald goes further. He extends the metaphor.

The valley becomes a “fantastic farm where ashes grow like wheat.” Death is spreading. Farmers are *growing* ashes. Ashes come alive.

And who is sowing the seeds? The rich malefactors on both sides of the valley. Nick, Tom, Gatsby, are all guilty. They aren't merely allowing it to happen. They are *farming* the ashes, actively cultivating this world of pollution and death. Later on, Myrtle dies in the valley trying to escape. Fitzgerald takes a description of highways and with it condemns all of New York society.

Now let's return to Richy's comparison of Clara to a rocket ship. "Now that she's blasted off, who knows where she'll land?"

What kind of maniac haphazardly launches rocket ships and watches to see where they'll land? Inherent to launching a rocket is knowing its trajectory. How does it speak well of St. George's if we shot Clara into outer space without any kind of mission control monitoring her from the ground?

(May 2019, continued)

Q: What did Jay Gatsby call baseball?
A: Old Sport.

(February 2007)

The technology of the Everything Bracelet wasn't different from that of any of the million smartphones, tablets, and watches everyone has now, but at the time it felt futuristic. Still, I didn't understand the check-in feature. Why would you want people to know where you were if you weren't picking up your phone when they called? And how would other people's data determine your sleep or eating habits? More important: I'd never seen a single person wearing one of these things.

My initial thought after reading the *Wired* article was that at least Clara was smart enough to refuse to sit for an interview. My second was that she'd only become more sought after. Everyone loves a genius who shies away from the spotlight.

And sure enough, a few weeks after the *Wired* profile came out, *People* magazine did two pages on her, depicting her as a simple kid with a big idea. She dressed in a red velour Adidas tracksuit and leaned against a CEO desk with her Everything Bracelet the focus of the camera.

She sat for an interview with *People*, but not *Wired*. Why? Maybe she wasn't ready when *Wired* came along. Maybe she wanted a more general audience. Either way, after *People* came the full press junket. St. George's faculty members started reporting media sightings on a near daily basis. This was only a year or two after YouTube was up and running, so most of the sightings were on live TV. Then she was in *GQ* wearing the same tracksuit, this time in aquamarine, the Everything Bracelet matching her gunmetal-gray special-edition Prada leather sneakers, according to the description in small white letters (ADIDAS SWEATSUIT $550; SPECIAL-EDITION PRADA SNEAKERS $2,950). Then came articles she wrote for *The Atlantic* on "the value of wearables," "the importance of analytics," and "how founders need to be the faces of companies in growth mode." She guest-hosted a week of CNBC's daily morning show, moderating debates about Silicon Valley's most over- and underappreciated companies. "Will VMware take flight? The answer after a brief commercial break." On the air she was bold and confident in her opinions, but her affect was flat. She was not herself. She was TV Clara. She wore TV makeup and had her hair done by TV stylists. She looked directly into the camera and made predictions sound like inevitabilities. VMware *would* take flight. I had no idea what she was talking about. Each morning, she wore a different velour Adidas tracksuit but spoke in an understated manner, as though she were reading off a teleprompter, even when in normal conversation.

We emailed around clips and clippings, proud of her, of ourselves, of St. George's. I confess to feeling pride. I was proud of her writing in *The Atlantic*. It didn't have any of the playfulness of her veal-on-a-plate essay or her answers on the Ember, but her prose was crisp and correct. I had taught her well.

If her perfect score on the Ember had planted the seed of Clara in my psyche, her fame germinated that seed into a forest. Something about an intimate's fame gets into you. It blossoms into a fascination. Or at least it did for me. From what I've since read about the phenomenon, my experience was common. There tend to be recognizable stages: surprise, followed by pride in parents and teachers or resentment in friends and classmates, followed by a desire that others know that *you* know the real person while those others just know the version presented to the public. The real Clara was playful, thoughtful, and a little bit dangerous. Media Clara was, above all else, competent. She had an idea. She executed it. She seemed to know about whatever new idea was laid before her. The articles about her, those she wrote, the television and NPR versions of Clara, were of, about, and by a different person than the one I knew. They were glossy and appealing and a little bit embarrassing. They were a performance. And it can be off-putting to see someone you know well perform. It's something like the phenomenon of the uncanny valley: As a robot's resemblance to a human increases, so does a viewer's affection for it, but only until the robot looks *almost* human. At that moment, it unnerves the viewer. I was increasingly thrilled for Clara until the point when I became unnerved by her. She was Clara and not-Clara. I began to look away.

(June 2007)

And then the profile in the *New York Times Magazine* headlined "Don't Come Looking for Me" that began: "By the time you read these words, Clara Hightower will be gone. Why? Because she doesn't like selling hardware, hosting television shows, or writing essays. Her time, she says, can be better spent."

That quickly, it was over.

Part IV

Clara the Optimist

(February 2008)

A year after Clara's disappearance, I received a link to a YouTube video from Monsieur Lejeune. In the video, Clara spoke. To say it wasn't what I expected would be an understatement. It was hard to see what she looked like, as the camera, possibly an early smartphone, was far away from the podium, and the barn she was in—or it looked like a barn—was dimly lit. But she sounded like her eighth-grade self. More eloquent, but full of energy again. From what I could see, there were probably a few dozen people with her in the room. Regardless, the audio was clear. She spoke without notes, and passionately. The opposite of what she'd looked like on TV. She wore a gray or brown T-shirt. The clip seemed to begin after she'd been speaking for some time. She was absentmindedly petting some kind of dog and paused every few minutes to tuck her hair behind her ears.

(Another trigger warning here, this time for animal cruelty.)

* * *

"I've been thinking a lot about this problem. Most of us turn a blind eye because it is simply too painful, but now I'm begging you to stare directly into the horrible sun.

"I've chosen a half dozen of the thousands of possible examples, but more than that, I encourage you to do your own reading. Start with *Animal Liberation* and take to heart Peter Singer's utilitarian vision. Humans force animals to suffer in unimaginable ways. That statement is inarguable. No one denies it. But very few people do anything to prevent it.

"When I refer to the unimaginable scale of animal suffering, I mean both the quantity of animals that are made to suffer and the extent to which individual animals suffer. We can't fathom the psychological pain. What does it mean that a chicken is sad? I don't know, and from what I understand, we're still far off from a true sense of how animal brains process sadness, loneliness, and fear. But that they experience physical pain — physical torture — there is no question. Physical pain we can see in their panic, impulses to flee or attack. We see physical pain in their twisted muscles and tormented cries.

"Singer is right to accuse most humans of an unforgivable speciesism. Animal suffering should be viewed through a prism of pain experienced as opposed to the animal's intelligence. We do everything we can to save a mentally challenged human toddler from physical pain, so for what logical reason would we not do the same for a pig whose intelligence and sense of pain more or less mirror the former's?

"So as I list the horrors we force animals to suffer, imagine those same things done to, say, your three-year-old nephew with developmental delays or your eighty-five-year-old grandfather with advanced Alzheimer's. And then imagine that same suffering endured by fifty billion three-year-old nephews with developmental delays or grandfathers with dementia each year.

"Did you know it's common practice for chickens to be prophylactically mutilated so they don't mutilate each other? Farmers routinely crack off their claws and beaks. Why? Because otherwise the chickens attack each other and damage the meat. Did you know chickens are force-fed in cages stacked dozens high? In their entire lives, they never see sunlight; they shit on each other and are shat on until they are slaughtered for their unnaturally large breasts and wings. Under these conditions, if farmers don't crack off the claws and beaks, chickens routinely puncture the flesh of their siblings.

"Maybe you didn't know it before, but you know it now. So I ask you: What are you going to do about it?"

At this point the camera — or phone, whatever it was — zoomed in, and I could see Clara's face. Her blue eyes flashed through the screen. Her hair was blonder than I remembered it. I hadn't been able to tell what type of dog she was absentmindedly petting, but now that I got a closer look, I thought it might be a goat or, more likely, a sheep.

"I could keep listing animals, but instead I'd like you to focus for a moment on slaughterhouses. Slaughterhouses are torture chambers for animals and humans. Cows are killed by metal bolts to the brain that often don't impale them properly the first time, so they moan until they are impaled again. Then they are hooked to a ceiling conveyor-belt system that brings them from station to station, where their blood is let and each body part chopped off one by one, and many are still alive during the process. Stunned, still suffering cattle, hanging upside down, watch as their own legs are hacked off their bodies, the first hack often not strong enough to take the limb off cleanly. And yet we do nothing.

"And then there's the human toll. First on the workers themselves. The chemicals used to clean most slaughterhouses are so toxic that slaughterers and meat packers cannot stay in the job for more than six months before their skin starts to peel off and their cardiac or lung capacity diminishes. Traditional soaps and disinfectants are not strong enough to remove the blood and oils from the factory floor and prevent bacteria, so instead of soaps and disinfectants, acids and bleaches are mixed and employed in concentrations that are dangerous to breathe. These mixtures inevitably get in the lungs, bloodstreams, boots, and gloves of the humans who work with these animals.

"Additionally, slaughterhouses *report* an average of more than one worker death or serious injury per month due to the weight and danger of the machines and knives used to carve these animals up as quickly as they come through. Most packers are in the country illegally so they have no one to complain to and no way to fight back when wages are withheld. Some work as slaves, kept in quarters not much cleaner or larger than those of the animals they are paid a dollar or two an hour to mutilate, torture, kill, and butcher. And yet we do nothing; we do nothing."

The sheep pressed its head into her hip, and she pressed back. Someone from the front row stood up and wrangled it out of the picture.

"But the human toll extends far beyond those men and women tasked with the killing. Animals kept in such tight quarters, eating soy and corn their bodies aren't built to consume, get sick quickly, and because they're packed so tightly together, illness spreads with unfathomable speed. So antibiotics are — "

The video cut off. What remained was the ghost of the grainy visual, Clara's confidence, her hands ably slicing up and down, back and forth, across the screen. It was thrilling to watch her teach.

(February 2008, continued)

Richy burst into the faculty lounge, which the year before had been renovated, repainted, and furnished with a bright white table, fluorescent lights, giant whiteboards on the walls, a gleaming toaster and a coffee maker, a retro pinball machine, a stainless-steel sink, straight-backed white chairs, a black leather sofa, and MacBook Pros. But no amount of bright light and metal could smother a century of sweat, desperation, and cafeteria soup.

When he saw Enid and me, he said, "Oh, fuck you both to hell."

"Richard?" Enid said.

We'd been sitting in silence, Enid eating her salad, me drinking tea and gnawing through a toasted cafeteria bagel.

"We've all seen it. And my cousin's guy in San Francisco confirms she's out. It's over," Richy said.

"Who?" I said, even though I knew. I wanted him to say her name.

"You're surprised?" Enid said.

"My cousin says his guy out there says she's persona non grata," Richy said. "Broken too many promises costing too many people too much money. He has it on good authority that she's changed her phone number. Isn't working for or with anyone. The animal bullshit is apparently her life now."

"Isn't it wonderful?" Enid said.

"I'm in no mood, Enid," Richy said. "Really. I'm...I don't know what to say." He circled the table and slowly sat down on the black leather sofa. He was fighting back tears. I took no joy in seeing him like this.

"After all I did for her," he said. "Taking care of her. Making sure Blink took her under his wing. The free tuition and books, backpacks, money for the science fair, for summer meals. The calls to guarantee her admission to Swarthmore."

"Richy," I said.

"Okay," he said, stifling a sob. "That's not what matters. It's not about the money. It's the lost potential. It's everything she could have had. Could have been. Could have given us. That selfish fucking— "

"Stop it," Enid said.

Richy turned to make sure the door was closed. "It's just us three here," he replied with real spite. "People have obligations. She's an adult. We had a lot riding on her. I personally did. I took care of her. We all did. We were her family. And she ran off because it got too hard? Because it wasn't what she wanted?"

"She must have been unhappy," Enid said.

"People are unhappy sometimes," Richy said. "They manage."

"She owed us nothing," Enid said.

"Oh, shut up," Richy said. "Don't you see? Don't you see that all the time, money, reputation...you didn't do any of that. I did that. Don't you see that it's for nothing now? She was our best hope at relevance. She was going to be what separated us from the rest of the tier B independent schools everyone laughs at. How am I going to tell Patty? Oh!" He sobbed in a deep breath. "And the board? How am I going to tell the board?"

"You're a ridiculous man," Enid said.

"Try to be kind," I said. "Both of you."

We three sat there as quietly as we could, breathing, composing ourselves. I shared Enid's relief at Clara getting out. But also, even after not interacting with Clara for close to a decade, I felt a preposterous twinge of dejection in response to Clara not having asked me for advice.

(November 2019)

We human beings are all a mishmash of greatness and littleness. Some have more strength of character or more opportunity and so in one direction or another give their instincts freer play, but in terms of potential, we are the same. Clara is no better than I am. I am no better than you. Caroline might be better than us all, but it is more likely that for some psychological or animal reason, the scent from her body gives me comfort. It reminds me of my mother's or its opposite. For my part I don't think I'm any better or any worse than anyone else, but I know that if I chronicled every action I've taken or thought that's crossed my mind, most people would consider me a monster of depravity. Our thoughts are ugly, vicious, lascivious, violent, terrified things. In our brains we are all animals. We are human only in our ability to suppress or, at the very least, not act on our thoughts.

Caroline tells me she's no longer interested in sex. I don't believe her, but it's kind of her to say. I tell her I have no problem with her pursuing that kind of thing with another man, but she knows I don't mean it.

"How does it feel to love a man whose body is broken but whose thoughts can still be communicated?" I ask her.

She responds that she loves me, that I am me, that it is no different than if I had a broken foot or a bad burn across my face.

I tense my unburned face to indicate that I don't believe her.

"I'm here, aren't I?" she says.

(February 2008, continued)

Christophe Lejeune tells me that in Silicon Valley, to "Hightower it out of here" still denotes having one's moment and then choosing to disappear. It works, perhaps, because of the sonic similarities between *hightail* and *Hightower.* In a world of Gateses, Zuckerbergs, Musks, Bezoses, and Huffingtons who try to hang around forever, Clara left at the beginning of her ascent.

Back then and still, it was Clara's escape from influence that was more impressive to me than her accrual of it. It is rare to enter the highest echelons of power. It is nearly unheard of to abandon them. Cincinnatus, George Washington, and Clara Hightower.

I didn't teach her coding, engineering, design, publicity, or marketing. But I did my best to teach Clara to become the best version of herself. Everyone asked why she would flee, but this was the same girl who'd stolen the crystal penguins. The same girl who'd thrown Darin's phone out the window. The same girl who'd aced the Ember as she made fun of it. Who'd broken up with the love of her life. A victory without subversion was never a real victory.

(March 2011, continued)

Three years had passed since we'd lost track of Clara. Enid invited Caroline, me, Harold Hopkins, Harold Hopkins's wife, and a dozen others to a small gathering in celebration of Jacob's engagement to a young woman named Skye. The apartment was the same except that what had been Jacob's bedroom was now Enid's studio, and there were only a few scattered crystal animals left. I asked Enid where the other crystals were, and she said, "Don't you ever tire of yourself?"

I told her no one was more tired of me than I was, but she'd already turned to introduce Skye to some arriving guests. I'd never seen Enid in this mode before: the soon-to-be-mother-in-law hostess, fluttering about, refilling drinks, presenting her son's striking new fiancée with the pride of an artist contemplating her creation. Enid looked happy. She looked old. I was old too.

And Skye was something. Dyed-black hair, fire-engine-red lipstick, black eyeliner. She dressed as a young person dresses when trying to look more mature. She wore a black pearl amulet necklace, silver and black rings that snaked around her fingers, and a sheer black halter top that showcased the tattoo that covered her right arm: red roses growing off green thorny stalks behind a black wrought-iron gate. The overall effect of the makeup, jewelry, clothes, and tattoo was that Skye looked far younger than her youthful round face and round brown eyes would have suggested on their own. She was in her late twenties but looked like a senior in high school.

"She's at the Icahn School of Medicine at Mount Sinai," Enid told each guest after letting them take a look. "She's leaning toward radiation oncology."

Jacob was planning to open a small restaurant in Brooklyn. Of course he was. He'd wanted to cook ever since he'd made me those pretend meals twenty years before. He had his same translucent skin, full lips, and bony nose, but his posture was better and his hair was cut close on the sides and brushed back on top in a style that was popular at the time. He had been working out. Lifting weights. Or his muscles had finally caught up with his bones. Though most guests dressed formally, Jacob wore jeans and a hooded zip sweater. He was very handsome.

"They look like lead singers in a rock band," I whispered to Caroline.

"Or avant-garde architects," Caroline said.

"Good band name," I said.

Enid made a toast:

"From the moment I met Skye, it was clear that she was the one for Jacob. If I had not been introduced to her yet and was asked to pick her out from a crowd of people, I would have been able to spot her right away. And I would have known she was Jacob's soulmate."

"Hurrah!" we all said. "Cheers!"

Skye's parents were staid midwestern people. They answered my questions but didn't ask me any. I congratulated Jacob on the restaurant and the engagement. I asked follow-up questions on both, and he let me know politely that he had other people to talk to but would love to grab a drink the following weekend.

(March 2011, continued)

Jacob suggested the Grassroots Tavern on St. Marks Place. This was the evening he told me about going to bed with Clara in eighth grade. At that moment, the story didn't seem as inappropriate or out of place as I presume it did in my retelling. Even all these years later, Jacob wanted to assert his closeness to Clara. My guess is that episode in the stairwell was one of the most important moments of his life, something he'd frequently relived, and especially now that he had committed his future to another woman, there weren't many people he could share it with. It's possible I was the only one. Also, as I might have mentioned earlier, students tend not to talk to former teachers, but when they do, everything comes pouring out. It's one of the unanticipated but lovely perks of the job. It's an honor to be momentarily let back into their world. I hadn't taught Clara or Jacob in a decade and a half, and in many ways I'd been living in the shadow of their eighth-grade year. Enid kept me up to date on Jacob, and I told my students about Clara. But Caroline wasn't interested, and Richy couldn't stand to hear her name anymore.

* * *

It was a marvelous evening for me, and for Jacob, I think, as well. We both said and drank too much. In trying to meet his level of candor, I told him that I'd loved his mother when we were together, that I was sad for her that she'd raised him without his father present most of the time, that I wish I'd done more for him but hadn't known how to without overstepping, and that I remained very curious about what Clara was up to. I mentioned the video, but he hadn't seen it.

"I don't think about her now as much as I used to," he said when he returned with another pitcher of Bud or Bud Light or maybe it was Coors or Miller Lite or Yuengling. "Last time I saw you was when my mother gave that insane commencement speech, right? That was at the end of our freshman year of high school, and though I was trying to keep my shit together, I was as much a mess as Mom was. You could probably tell. That year — to be honest, the first couple years of high school — I spent mourning Clara. I kept thinking she'd come back to me. That she'd turn against the trust-fund poseurs at Dalton and come back to me. I called her once in a while when I couldn't take it anymore, but I stopped that after my mother pointed out, totally correctly, that she — Mom, I mean — could tell whenever I let myself call or see Clara because I'd be depressed for weeks after."

"Do you have any idea how Clara is doing?" I asked. "Is she okay?"

"I think so," he said. "We text, but she doesn't give me details. Of course I saw all the articles — 'Can't Catch Clara,' 'Don't Come Looking for Me.' I've heard that she's still working on some venture-capitalist-funded secret project to change the way we all interact with one another. But I've also heard she's tending cattle on a farm somewhere away from the rest of the world. I don't ask her, which is why I think she still reaches out sometimes. I know she's cut a lot of people off."

"But is she still Clara?" I said.

"What?" he said.

"You text with her regularly?" I said.

"Not really. I haven't told her yet about Skye."

I drank. He drank. He was a chef. I'd taught him how to write. That made me feel good. I didn't know what to say.

"You maintained contact with Clara in high school," I said.

"I mean, yes, but it wasn't like I didn't have friends in high school," he said.

I don't know if people in their late twenties are adults yet. I don't know if anyone is ever really an adult.

"I even eventually had some girlfriends," he said. "Or girls that I hooked up with. But when I think back on the first couple years of high school, mostly I remember playing mind games with myself, telling myself that if I fell asleep early and left my ringer on, Clara would call me and wake me, or if I stayed in the shower longer, she'd call me, or if I got out of the shower too soon, she might not call, or if I left our answering machine off, I wouldn't be so disappointed that there wasn't a message or, even worse, if there was a message and it wasn't from her. If my machine was on, I had to come home and be disappointed, but if it was off I knew I had nothing to disappoint me. I had trouble sleeping. Trouble following along in my classes. I didn't eat, or I would eat an entire box of doughnuts. I didn't study, but I got good grades because high school was so much easier than middle school. I didn't really care that much about new friendships. I started smoking weed. Weed helped. So did drinking. Most weekends I got wasted with Eric."

"Eric from St. George's?" I said. Eric was the husky boy in the Yankees cap whom Clara had forbidden to clear the table that day in the cafeteria.

"Yeah. He hated his high school too. He's good now. He joined the Marines. Did four tours in Iraq and is now in some kind of venture-capital fund."

"Four?"

"He does those Ironman races. Skye loves him. She's always trying to set him up with her friends."

"And in high school you got wasted with him," I said.

"Ha, yeah," he said. "Not like partying or anything, just vodka and orange juice in my room till we passed out. Pretty sad, looking back. And he rolled the most perfect blunts — remember blunts?"

I couldn't say that I did.

"That was a lot of high school for me, just floating outside myself or waking up with a headache on a pile of towels in the bathroom. And the rest of the time, I cooked."

I must have given him a quizzical look, because he said, "You remember — of course you remember — I've always been into cooking. Mom never cooked," he continued, "but she had all these old cookbooks. *The Joy of Cooking. Mastering the Art of French Cooking. The Moosewood Cookbook.* I didn't want to be out in case Clara came by, but I had nothing to do at home. Mom was teaching or working at a studio she shared with some other artists, and after school on the days she taught, she stayed and used the school kiln for her own stuff. She was crazy with work back then, constant work, and there were only so many Eminem and Spice Girls music videos I could watch without making myself crazy. I thought a lot about sex. Sex with Clara. I missed sex. I was so angry at everything, so I'd make a salad and roast a chicken. It was calming. Contemplative. It helped me not think. Assembling the ingredients, chopping, mixing wet and dry, tinkering with recipes, starting over, perfecting, finding fresh herbs and spices at the farmers' market or Indian shops off Sixth Street. I couldn't focus on books or in class. When I was cooking and when I was drunk or high — those were the only times I didn't think about Clara.

"And it was nice to eat with Mom at the end of the day. She would come home exhausted. People always used to tell me I was the man of the house, and I never knew what that meant, but it was nice to be able to feed her. We didn't talk much, but it felt like home, the two of us. I got really into desserts. Cookies, cakes, but then galettes, pies, tarts."

My beer was cold and light. *Life is difficult*, I thought. People try to tell stories in ways that make themselves seem as if they were more perceptive than they'd actually been at the time. People try to tell stories about other people but end up talking about themselves.

"I've heard that people make their closest friends in high school," Jacob said, "and I wonder if I missed out on that because of Clara. If my whole life could have been different and maybe much better if we hadn't dated in eighth grade.

"Eighth grade!" He banged the table. "We were so young. It's so embarrassing that I'm still talking about my eighth-grade girlfriend like this. I'm about to get married!"

"Skye seems great," I said.

"But I don't blame myself. I had something wonderful and I lost it, so it was hard for me to focus on my geometry test or making friends on the basketball team or whatever when there was this bigger key to my happiness who lived two floors above me."

I seized the moment: "She could have been in the same school. Mr. Madison kept you two apart. Didn't recommend you to Dalton."

"I never could have gotten in even if he had," Jacob said.

"No, you were close," I said. "Very close. But Mr. Madison felt it'd be worse for you to be together."

"I've always hated that guy," Jacob said. "But there's no way I would have survived Dalton. I don't think anyone does. And living near her was hard enough. Imagine our being in the same classes?"

"But you would have stayed together," I said.

"She'd already broken up with me by then."

"But maybe she wouldn't have if she'd known you were going on to high school together."

"Yeah, maybe," he said.

This was the conversation I'd been waiting to have for more than ten years. Finally I could prove Richy wrong. But Jacob didn't care.

I'd been holding this grudge against Richy for preventing Jacob and Clara from being together, but there was never a single reason for the dissolution of their relationship. There were an infinite number of reasons. Don't misunderstand me: Richy didn't deserve forgiveness. He'd been wrong. But I realize now that that didn't mean I'd been right.

"School aside, living in the same building was a big part of why I couldn't stop thinking about Clara," he said. "And she still had the key to our place as far as I knew, so anytime I heard someone walking down the stairs, especially when I heard or thought I heard RJ, or anytime the phone rang, or on those days when I lingered by the subway exit for a few extra minutes, I let myself feel hope. All I had to do was knock or call. I couldn't face her in person without crying, so sometimes in the morning I called."

* * *

I was feeling drunk. My thoughts sped and then slowed. I reined myself in. I sat on my hands to calm myself. I took a deep breath. In through the nose for four, feel my belly fill up; out through the mouth for six, feel my lips flutter. He didn't seem to be taken aback by my overreaction.

He continued, "She always picked up on the first ring, which I didn't know how to interpret. Was she waiting for me to call, just as I was waiting for her to, or did she have another person who was calling her? So too often I wheedled and bargained and acted pathetic. Like I'd say, 'Let's be together but we only see each other one Saturday per month and that one day will be the best day of the month for you and me and RJ,' and she'd point out all the reasons that plan would make us both miserable, and she didn't want to humor me, and she didn't think she'd ever want to get married, but in twenty years, if she did want to get married, then, yes, we should reconnect and see how things were going, see if we both wanted kids or if there was another logical reason to get married, and again, I rejoiced that she still wanted to be with me, and I was miserable because she was clearly just blowing me off. And also, I knew that my being so needy would make her love me less."

"You should tell her you're getting married," I said. "Maybe she's still counting on that twenty-year plan."

He smiled sadly at me.

"Six more years," he said, and was quiet for a moment before seeming to shake himself out of a reverie and continuing. "A nice thing about getting engaged is that I'm closing that door for good. Now no part of me expects Clara to call one day and say that twenty years have passed and maybe we should talk about getting married."

"You think she remembers?"

"Yes," he said.

"You're sure," I said.

"Yes."

"Did you talk a lot about it back then?"

"She avoided me. Until suddenly she called. RJ had died. Hit by a motorbike. The guy on the bike was hurt too. It was no one's fault. These things happen. But she was responsible for our dog. It was her fault. I got so angry."

"I bet!" I said.

I controlled myself. I couldn't get over the dog. I don't know why. Maybe because I was there in the beginning. He was such a sweet thing. I don't even like dogs, really. I don't want to live with them. I don't like forcing them to live with people. They run away. You give dogs food and shelter every day and then you have to tie them up or else they'll run away. They don't want to be with you. The whole thing seems selfish to me. But RJ was different. I'd held him in my hands when he was only a few weeks old.

"One day toward the end of junior year, I think," he said, "I accused Clara of lying to me about being single, and she, in her cool, infuriating way, looked me in the eye and told me that yes, she was seeing someone, but she hadn't lied to me — she'd never said otherwise. She said that if I hadn't been 'performatively distant' with her, she would have told me earlier. Said that she was glad I'd asked, as she didn't want me to hear it from anyone else, but she had a boyfriend, and though they mostly hung out inside school, they really were boyfriend and girlfriend and that she was sorry but didn't know what to say.

"And when I broke down crying and called her a fucking bitch who'd ruined my entire life, she said she knew she'd acted terribly and that she didn't know why or what had changed, but she thought she might be happy and productive with this guy in a way she couldn't be happy and productive with me. She told me she hadn't ruined my life. She said we were only sixteen years old, and we'd been together when we were only thirteen and that we had seventy more years of life ahead of us so I should stop blaming her for doing something that everyone did to everyone else all the time."

A bartender dropped some glasses, and everyone cheered.

The bartender shouted, "Go fuck yourselves!" and we cheered again.

The Grassroots Tavern has been closed since before my stroke, but what a place that was. A dollar for a basket of popcorn, eight dollars for a pitcher of cold beer. Wooden floors and dusty walls and round tables, square booths, classic rock, darts in the back. NYU kids, drunks at the bar, folks like us stopping in for a conversation.

We sat in silence for a minute or two. We took turns using the bathroom.

"Your mom mentioned you still saw her sometimes during those days," I said.

"What do you mean?" he said.

"At night?" I said.

Jacob flinched, then stiffened.

"That's between me and Clara," he said.

What happened in the stairwell was one thing. For whatever reason, their nights together post breakup were something else.

* * *

"Sorry," I said. I pivoted. "It must have been good to get away for college," I said.

"She checked in on me on my birthday and when the Yankees won the World Series. High school was hard. Emotionally, I mean. But not college. I majored in communications. No one could write as well as I could, thanks to you. Essays, but creative writing too. I took a bunch of creative-writing classes. I still remember the rules you taught us for the Ember. The BILES comma method: beginner, interrupter, linker, expander, separator. Prepositions were 'anywhere a mouse can go,' like *over, under, around.* All that stuff stuck. College was great, actually…"

Did his remembering the comma and preposition rules fill me with a dizzying joy? Of course it did. But I was drunk and already heading toward dizzy.

"I worked in the cafeteria," Jacob said, "and then got a job cooking at an Italian restaurant where parents took their kids when they visited them at school. And then, through Mr. Madison, actually, I got a job in the kitchen at Café Boulud, and that was where I met people, got funding, was able to set up my own place. Skye's family has money, so I have a couple years' cushion before my restaurant fails like they all eventually do. Or maybe mine won't! I'm good. I can cook. Skye wants to hire a publicist. Did you meet her? Isn't she great?"

"She is great! Really smart, pretty. But wait. Mr. Madison got you a job with Daniel Boulud?"

"Yeah, wasn't that great of him?"

"It was," I said. "He never mentioned it to me." *That overcome-by-*

guilt son of a bitch needed to find a way to make up for his treachery! Ha! I thought. *Ha, ha, ha!*

"I guess he knew I didn't want it getting around to people that it was connections that got me where I am."

"I guess," I said, drunker than I'd realized.

"Skye is pretty, isn't she?" Jacob said.

"Did you tell her about Clara?" I said.

"Tell who?"

"Telos!" I shouted and started to laugh. I was very, very drunk.

"What telos?"

"Your telos is to love Clara!" I said. My stomach hurt, I was laughing so much. He started to laugh too.

"Skye," he said. "Telos?"

"Tell us!" I was laughing so hard, I was full-on crying.

"Us?"

"Her? Tell Skye!"

"Tell her what?" he said, catching his breath. He'd stopped laughing and was crying now. But not from laughter. He was just crying. "That I'm still obsessed with my eighth-grade girlfriend? That I've spent the past three hours talking about that girlfriend to my middle-school English teacher? That even though I just asked Skye to spend the rest of her life with me, I'd leave her in a second if it meant I could be with Clara? No, I didn't tell Skye."

"Do you think she knows?" I said, calming myself down.

He didn't answer that; he seemed to have shifted into a different register. He stood up, went to get us a fresh pitcher. He wanted Clara. She was his family. Skye was by all accounts a smart, caring, pretty, capable girl. But Jacob loved Clara. I knew it.

Jacob returned, set the pitcher between us, and exaggeratedly stretched his arms above his head and yawned.

"I'm calm now," he said. "Sorry. I love Skye. She loves me. We're in love! I'm going to open the restaurant, and Skye will be a doctor, and we'll have kids," Jacob said. "My wife will be a hot, brilliant doctor, and she will love me, and we'll have a great life together. Maybe we should get married at the restaurant."

"That's great," I said. "Really great. I'm really happy for you." Jacob drained his glass quickly and filled us both back up. I noticed just then that the bar smelled like piss.

"Knock-knock," Jacob said.

"Who's there?"

"Do you want two CDs?" he said.

"Do you want two CDs who?" I said.

"Do you want two CDs nuts?" he said.

I don't remember much else after that, just that over the course of the evening, my allegiances shifted from Clara and Enid to this boy who'd never gotten over a girl.

(March 2011, continued)

"You stink of beer," Caroline said later that night as she rolled away from me after I kissed her neck. I pulled her closer.

"My love!" I declared. "Let me put French fries in your ears!"

She punched me in the stomach.

"Ow!" I said. I smiled in the dark.

"You!" Punch. "Stink!" Punch. "Of!" Punch. "Beer!"

"We don't do this!" I said. "This punching of me is not a thing we do!"

"Go to sleep," Caroline said. "I'm tired and you stink."

"My love!" I said.

Now that I'm years past being able to sleep with Caroline, the moments I think of with her are not so much the times we slept together as the times when we could have done so. The possibility, the wondering if she was wondering. That's what I find myself thinking about more than the act itself.

"Go to sleep," Caroline said that night.

I rolled over and hugged my pillow.

"I love you too," I said.

"What do you mean, *too*?" Caroline said.

"Then I love you, period," I said.

"I love you too," she said.

I love you too.

(June 2011)

I was surprised not to be invited to the wedding. But maybe they had it at Jacob's restaurant and had room only for immediate family. I was surprised that my phone calls to Jacob went unanswered, and I thought of all the ways I might have offended him during our evening together. I stayed away from the restaurant. Caroline told me I was being silly. The logic of his ignoring me was obvious, she said. I reminded him of Clara, and his life was not sustainable if he kept thinking of Clara. Whether accurate or not, Caroline's argument was convincing enough to set my mind mostly at rest.

(December 2019)

Here's a goose joke I thought of over a week ago while I was lying in my hospital bed next to Caroline's healthy-person bed in our bedroom. I keep remembering it at night and forgetting to write it *down* (goose pun) until now:

> *Human: I like to consider myself a people person.*
> *Goose: I like to consider myself a geese goose.*

Caroline agrees with you. She didn't laugh either when I typed it out for her, but double goose in her eye. The joke works.

Part V

Clara the Archon

(August 2012)

In the summer of 2012, more than a year after that night at the Grassroots Tavern, Enid called to give me a message. We'd been calling each other lately. She was lonely. And I admit that I was too. Caroline wasn't interested in St. George's anymore. There had been too many students. Too many years. Caroline and I read on our elegant, comfortable beige couch. We sat close to each other. I read best when Caroline was near me. We went to bed with each other still. I picked her up at the bookstore and took her for sushi dinner. We talked about my day and hers. About Henry's latest invention. But I needed to talk about teaching too, and Enid was a good teacher, despite her claims that she was just using the gig to make her own art. Enid and I talked about our students. But this call was different. On this call, Enid told me that Clara wanted to meet. I asked where, and Enid named the most expensive restaurant in upstate New York. I laughed and told her to just give Clara my number. Enid replied that she had told Clara I wouldn't like this plan, but Clara had insisted, gave her the time and date, and said Caroline was welcome to come too.

"She sounded upset," Enid said. "You should go."

So I went.

Caroline and I did not usually go for fine dining, and for years this restaurant had been written up as the very finest: The chef's ancient techniques of French and Japanese gastronomy. The farm-to-table freshness. The heirloom seeds! I'm sure you've heard of these things. You take a tour of the farm and see the pigs and eggs and turnips and grapes before those very fauna and flora appear on your table. The meet-and-eat-the-meat concept had unnerved me the first time I saw a waiter at an upscale Chinatown restaurant take a sad lobster out of its tank, so the concept of petting a sheep and then gnawing on mutton did not appeal—especially at $550 per person, including wine pairings. Adding to that my dislike of hotels—and Caroline and I had to stay the night because neither of us could drive after so much paired wine—I thought about telling Enid to call Clara and cancel. But Clara needed me. She had chosen me for whatever this was. Of course I would be there.

Upon arrival, Caroline and I were taken on a tour by a fresh-faced boy somewhere between the ages of fourteen and forty. He led us through the chicken coops that somehow didn't smell like chicken shit and the rows of colorful vegetables that were, I must admit, beautiful.

I've never been one for natural beauty—sunsets, mountains, beaches. I prefer van Gogh's paintings of the field to the field itself. But the car rental and drive north and impending sleepless night on hotel pillows were all worth it for the pristine rows of potatoes, tomatoes, corn, melons, squash, and cucumbers. I realize for the first time now in writing this that it's unlikely all these crops could have been in season simultaneously, so perhaps my memory is wrong, or the produce was fake, or maybe the magic manure from their organic-grass-fed luxury swine made possible the coexistence of swelling tomatoes in purple, green, and red beside large and small melons, squashes flecked by a white that glowed gold in the sunset. And all of it in front of a mile of corn. Miraculous, that so much wild beauty could be contained and combined and visually curated. Closer to art than nature.

And dinner was very good. It was fine. It was certainly above average. The floor was hardwood, the aesthetic somewhere between Chelsea art gallery and billionaire's farmhouse. The salads were fresh and nice to look at, and the bread and butter were good, though good bread has little to do with a farm. The fish tasted like fish, but we were trashed by then anyway. Moreover, it was difficult to concentrate on the meal because it had started to feel like some kind of elaborate prank. Clara was teasing an old teacher into spending a thousand dollars on dinner. Or if not Clara, Enid. Enid had known I would go if she mentioned Clara. But Caroline and I hadn't been out to a truly nice meal in years. We committed to enjoying it no matter what. And it turned out I was inventing injustices because with the kakuni came Clara.

(August 2012, continued)

Kakuni, our waiter explained, was Japanese pork belly simmered in sake, dashi, soy sauce, and mirin. Cooking the pork belly slowly over low heat broke the collagen down into gelatin that maintained the meat's moisture, ensuring a tenderness that allowed it to be consumed with chopsticks, which in our case had been cut earlier that day from a poplar tree on premises. The dish was traditionally served with scallions, daikon, and karashi but this evening would be accompanied by smoked pork sliders and a guanciale sausage served on a bed of mustard greens beside a short stack of puréed-then-pan-fried cannas.

Clara's face was thinner than I remembered, and her arms and shoulders were stronger. Otherwise, she hadn't changed much. Her body was calm, but her eyes shone. She wore work boots, jeans, and a Bernie Sanders pin on a thick wool sweater the same bright blue as her eyes.

I stood. "Well, if it isn't 'Can't Catch Clara' herself!" I said.

She didn't respond. Just looked at me with an open, curious expression.

"Sorry," I said.

"May I give you a hug?" she said.

I opened my arms and she put hers under mine and squeezed.

"Have a seat, have a seat," I said.

"It's so good to see you," she said as we sat.

"You too," I said. And it was. Clara! In the flesh.

"Hi, I'm Clara," she said to Caroline.

"Nice to meet you," Caroline said. "I've heard a lot about you over the years. Thanks for getting us the reservation. The meal has been lovely."

"It's all paid for," she said. "The GM owes me a favor. Multiple favors."

"You didn't need to," I said.

"I wanted to," she said. "I've missed you. How are you?"

I scanned the room. Half the diners were Clara's age; the men's stiff sports coats and open shirt collars suggested they worked in hedge funds or commercial real estate. The other half were clearly celebrating seventieth or eightieth birthdays.

The lack of rings on the fourth finger of Clara's left hand didn't mean she was single, as she didn't wear any jewelry at all, and her hair was pulled back in a way that suggested the physical impression she made on others wasn't high on her list of priorities. I was pleased to see she'd grown into herself. The last time I'd seen her in person, she'd been an awkward high-school kid. Now she looked confident. Not feminine like Caroline; not artificial like when she'd been on TV. More like Enid had been as a young woman.

"What can I do for you?" I said.

"Hold your horses," Clara said.

"My horses?" I said.

"Yes," she said. "Your horses."

"Giddyup," I said.

"That's the opposite of holding them," she said.

The warmth of my smile shot through my body. This was something. We were onto something.

"Consider them held," I said.

It was so good to see her. I looked down at my plate. I moved to take a bite but stopped myself. Her YouTube speech made it feel wrong to eat meat in front of her. Our table was a heavy slab of thick wood. No cloth. Just plates, glasses, silverware. No candle or flowers. It was large enough to easily accommodate the third chair in which Clara now sat, facing the white stucco wall.

On the drive up, Caroline and I had discussed what Clara might want. It wouldn't be money, unless she was truly desperate, and with all the people she knew in San Francisco, I wouldn't be the one to contact for cash. Caroline's guess was that it was something literary. She'd written the first draft of a book—a memoir or collection of essays—that she wanted me to take a look at. That seemed possible. But why not call or email me a manuscript? My fantasy, which I didn't dare disclose even to Caroline, was that Clara wanted my help thinking through the repercussions of, or putting the final touches on, some new piece of technology or way of living that she thought I'd have some unique perspective on. But dragging us out here most likely meant it had to do with something upstate. Maybe she had heard that things were changing at St. George's, figured that I was nearing retirement age, and so was inviting us to join some kind of commune or utopian community. As outlandish as it sounded, that had been my best guess. An invitation to join a community that she would show us that night or the next morning. And I was considering it: To, in my final decades, play the role of hoary eccentric among artists and retirees on a quest for inner peace. I would carry a walking stick and smoke Filipino cigars. I'd finally buy myself a flowing velvet cape.

But now that seemed unlikely.

"I'll let you know why I've asked you here, but then you'll have questions, and I'll need to answer them, so please, may I hear just a little about you first? How are you?"

How was I? I was fine. I was still teaching. Still married to the love of my life. Still reading, still perfecting the Ember. I'd held Henry's new baby a few months back.

"I'm great," I said. "Teaching. Still teaching."

"Is it true what they say about students?" she said. "That teachers keep getting older but students stay the same age?"

"No, they get younger," I said.

She laughed.

"You were the oldest," I said. "They've only gotten younger since you."

She laughed again, which made me laugh.

"Our only Archon ever," I said.

"You still do it?" she said.

"The Ember?" I said.

"Teach full-time," she said.

"Every day."

"You love it?" she said.

"Usually. There are days when I'm tired, but it beats a real job."

"You're downplaying how much you love it," she said.

I thought about it.

"I don't think I am," I said. "Compared to working on an assembly line or writing up PowerPoint presentations, sure."

"You'd be great at presentations," she said. "Explaining why a potential client should go with your firm."

"I'm no salesman," I said.

"That's exactly what you are." She paused. Then: "In the best possible way."

"You're the one selling bracelets," I said.

"For a couple of months," she said. "I couldn't take it." She looked up at me. "You know, I really have missed you. You and Enid. And Jacob. There aren't many people I miss."

"We missed you too," I said.

A pause in the conversation. The first awkward moment.

"And Caroline's son just had a son," I said. "I'm a step-grandparent!"

"How wonderful," Clara said to Caroline. "I didn't know you had a son. Congratulations!"

"But I want to hear about you," I said. "I've followed you from afar."

"Enid has told me as much."

"We all root for you," I said.

"And I appreciate that," Clara said. "Enid and I talk, as you know. But it stays superficial. I love her. She's more like a mom than my mom was."

"Why is it superficial?"

"She gets dismissive when I ask about her. Says she wants to hear about me. That there's nothing to say about herself. And I can't ask her about Jacob," she said. "Is he doing well, as far as you know? Is he really married?"

"He is," I said. "Skye is great."

"That makes me so happy," she said.

"Does it?" I said.

"Stop it," Caroline said. I'd forgotten Caroline was there.

"Caroline is right," Clara said. "Stop it. Of course it makes me happy."

(August 2012, continued)

Clara excused herself to go to the restroom. With her gone for a few minutes, Caroline and I did our best to eat. I thought Caroline might say something about Clara, but she didn't. And I didn't know what to say. The kakuni was slimy, the canna nearly too dense to chew. But the guanciale sausage, the size and shape of a double-A battery, was ethereally good. It hit every taste bud. Thinking back, I can say that it was the last great bite of my life.

The tables closest to ours felt miles away. The music was barely audible. Caroline wasn't eating her guanciale sausage. She said she didn't want it, that she was full. I was full too, but come on! I reached across the table to stab it, but Clara rejoined us.

"Okay," she said.

"Okay," I said.

"I'm going to ask you for something," she said.

"I figured as much," I said.

"I always knew I could ask for your help and you would never judge me," she said. "You are the person I've always thought of when

I need something. To be honest with you, I am in a little trouble. I can't tell you why. I might have pushed things too far. But I need to say I was with you at a certain time. I do hope you won't ask too many questions. You'll let this go?"

"Of course you can say you were with me," I said.

"Let her explain first," Caroline said. "You can't promise anything yet."

"Caroline is right," Clara said. "But it's nothing too serious. As long as I can tell them I was in the city with you."

"Tell who?" Caroline said.

"The Federal Bureau of Investigation," she said.

I laughed a big ugly laugh. But it was a funny line! In my entire life, I don't think I'd ever heard anyone call the FBI by its full name with such sincerity and nonchalance.

And though I should have been thinking about what trouble she'd gotten into, what had been done to or by her, what she was asking me to risk on her behalf, my only thought at the moment was that the very best one of them had come back to me.

(August 2012, continued)

Of all the incidents both meaningful and meaningless that I now spend my life remembering — the rippling curtains of my nursery maid's room, my mother's death and father's departure, my first moments with Caroline at the bookstore, meeting her son, our wedding, my successes and failures in the classroom — I spend as much time on this conversation as any other.

I was about to tell Clara again that yes, of course I'd lie for her, but I grew dizzy. I finished my glass of wine. Pulled myself together. Sat on my hands. Took a deep breath.

Or maybe I'm just struggling to breathe now. In through the nose for four, et cetera. It's supposed to calm me down, but breathing like this reminds me of all the other times in my life I've been anxious enough to need to remind myself to breathe like this, so it now has the opposite effect. I breathe in through my nose for four, out through my mouth for six, and my heart starts to race.

* * *

I so often think about this conversation because Clara gave me a gift by spending her time with me. Even by asking me for this favor. But also because Caroline blames Clara for what happened to me soon after, a contention both understandable and ludicrous. These past few years have been tremendously difficult for Caroline, and it's nice to have someone to blame. In Clara's defense, there's no reason to think I had the stroke because I went with her to Nebraska. But that's what one doctor said once, and Caroline has held on to that single unsubstantiated claim. That one doctor said that although my heart and arteries were vulnerable at the time, the stroke itself was probably stress-induced, and other than that trip to Nebraska I didn't have much stress in my life.

"I'm sure we can find some way to help you out," I told Clara at the dinner table.

"Hold on," Caroline said. "Stop it right now. Thanks for inviting us out here, but this is enough."

I wonder if Caroline is right, and if we'd walked away then, I wouldn't have had the stroke. How could I not wonder, during the long nights when I distract myself with memories, waiting for Caroline to wake up and tend to my body?

But the thing is: I was never going to stand up and walk away. Clara could have confessed to murder, and I would have at the very least stayed and listened. For so many years I'd been thinking about Clara and what had happened to her, and there she was in front of me. But in looking back now, I understand it was more than that. My retirement was looming. Maybe in a year, maybe in a few, but I knew it was coming soon. And I needed to have done something with my life. To have had some effect on some of my students.

Of the thousands of students I've taught, only a handful have come back to me as adults to tell me anything about what they became. The others might remember my name. Maybe they think of a funny moment in one of my classes or vaguely of the plot of a book they read with me. Maybe they'll remember a rule about grammar or usage — or a poem. They'll still have a few lines of "Spring and Fall: To a Young Child" in their minds. *It is the blight man was born for, / It is Margaret you mourn for.*

They'll remember the school friends they might still care about in some real way. They'll remember laughing with me or at me with those friends. But I will be a small part of a brief period in their lives at one of many schools they attended if they were lucky (or unlucky). Maybe I added some joy or brightness that lingered just long enough for them to find one right word at one right moment, to avoid a contentious conversation with a spouse or take a breath before shouting back on the subway.

I think of all of us who wanted to be meaningful in the lives of our students. Enid, Richy, Szilvia, Hopkins, even miserable, ichthyic Bruce. A student at St. George's had, on average, six teachers per year for core subjects, plus art, PE, dance, music, and drama teachers. Add to that division heads, learning specialists, school psychologists, kitchen staff, maintenance staff, security, and the nurse, and that's conservatively fifteen adult professionals who went to St. George's each day with the hope of improving students' lives. And those students were in school for an average of eighteen years, so even if they had slightly fewer adults in first grade and slightly more in tenth, that was still about 270 adults who had some hope of improving students' lives. And of those 270, how many did? Three? One? And what's the chance that, for my students, I was the one?

I needed at the very least to hear her out.

(August 2012, continued)

We three took turns looking at one another. Caroline was disquieted. Clara needed me. I didn't want to choose between them, but there was a thrill in being asked to. The silence lasted too long. The next logical step was for Clara to provide a better explanation of why she needed help, but she must have felt inhibited in front of Caroline, which Caroline understood before I did.

"If you'll excuse me," Caroline said. We hadn't had dessert, but it was late, after ten o'clock. I told her I'd walk her to the bed-and-breakfast, but she told me to stay, that she knew the way, the walk was short, the cool air would feel good, she was so happy to see me so happy, she was drunk and exhausted and excited to sleep. She hugged Clara and then me.

"Be careful," Caroline whispered in my ear. "It will be easier for you to say no without me here. Blame me. Say I'm too delicate to take on this kind of anxiety. Just don't agree to anything before we talk about it tomorrow," she said.

I nodded.

* * *

It wasn't unusual for Caroline to stand up and leave in the middle of a meal or conversation, even one that hadn't run so late. Caroline is the best, most desirable, intelligent, and attractive human being in the world, but she had and still has a certain frigidity to her, which I'm comfortable putting in writing because she and I have discussed it at length, and she knows it to be true. She calls it honesty; I call it selfishness or, as I just did, frigidity, but it is just one small part of who she is. It is the part that society least accepts in people—especially in women—but I've learned to live with it, to love it, even. If she didn't like me for some reason, she'd let me know she needed a week, for example, and she'd take it. We'd live together still, but we'd eat separately and not talk much. And then she'd come back. It helps me trust her love now, knowing she's disinclined to fake it.

I worry about Caroline, forced to be alone with me these days. She is growing critical. She complains of the occupational therapist's rough handling of me. She complains the food she orders is delivered cold. She doesn't tip in those cases, as though it's the delivery person's fault. In the early days right after the stroke, I would tense my face at her to indicate I thought she was being unreasonable. And when I started communicating through the screen, I would jibe her a bit—*Lay off*, I would write, or *I like cold soup*, or *Give him a break, he's working hard for hardly any money*—but I long ago stopped criticizing. That said, I fear that by not pushing and prodding her, I am not providing enough challenge. I write on my screen that she should do a sudoku, and she gets angry. She's got enough to do, she says, and of course she's right. Or she says something less kind. "I've got a lot to do just keeping you alive," she says. Or she'll use a word she knows I don't like, like *diaper.* "Feeding, bathing, diapering you."

She — you, I can write, in the second person — you need more than I am able to provide. I don't mind the occasional frigidity. You're kind far, far more often than you are cruel. But I don't know how to take care of you. Go out and see friends, if there are any you can still tolerate. Do the crossword puzzle, at least. Call Henry. Keep busy with things other than me. I don't love you merely for your good looks! Stay sharp. I need you sharp. I know I'm in no position to judge or ask anything more of you than you're already giving, but take care of yourself. I'll tell you that here, and you can read it as fiction if you'd like. It is fiction, if you want it to be.

I walked Caroline out of the restaurant and gave her upper arm a squeeze. She kissed me on the lips. She tasted drunk. I wanted to return with her to the room, but both our bellies were too full for that anyway, and who knew if I'd ever see Clara again.

I went back into the restaurant, to our table. I sat. The plates had been cleared, Clara's chair removed. She was now sitting across from me, in Caroline's place.

(August 2012, continued)

From Jacob, I'd heard about the painful end of their relationship. And RJ's death.

From Christophe Lejeune, I'd heard about her finding her way in the world.

I'd read about the Everything Bracelet and her disappearance.

From the YouTube video, I saw her concern for farmed animals.

From Enid, I'd heard that she needed my help.

But I wanted more. I wanted Clara to string these pieces of her life together in a way that made sense. That started from the girl I knew and brought me to this strange woman before me now.

Fiction needs causality. One thing must lead to the next. To use E. M. Forster's famous example, "The king died and then the queen died" is a story, whereas "The king died, and then the queen died of grief" is a plot. Novels need plot. We need one thing to happen *because* another thing did. That way, details matter. One scene not only precedes the next but also inevitably leads to it. That sort of causality creates meaning both in fiction and in real life, so I understand why I wanted it then and why Caroline still wants it now, but that's rarely the way real life works. I could not have predicted it at that table in upstate New York, but I did eventually go to Nebraska with Clara. I had a stroke. It ruined my life. Which ruined Caroline's life. But no doctor knows if I could just as easily have had the stroke grading essays or walking to school.

Also, dying of grief is something only fictional characters do. What's more likely is that the king died and the queen later succumbed to the same illness that took the king's life. Or the king died, and therefore the queen committed suicide. Would the queen have died if she'd been exercising more often? If she'd been eating more leafy greens, perhaps her immune system could have fought off the virus that killed the king, or perhaps she would have been more equipped to endure the depression that followed her husband's death.

I taught Clara. She tried to maximize her value for humans and other animals. Those are the facts. The rest is just emotion and conjecture.

I told Clara perhaps I could help her with the alibi if she helped me understand what she was going through, if she'd string the pieces of her life together in a way that made sense, but she waved me off.

"Tell me about Dalton," I said.

She ignored the question.

"I think a lot about you," she said. "How does someone become Mr. Keating? When you were a kid, did other kids ask you for help?"

"Are you asking if I was always like me or if I used to be like you?"

"I hadn't thought of it that way," she said.

Dessert was pickled blueberries, hazelnut bread pudding, and white chocolate and beer ice cream. *Sure,* I thought. *Why not? Pickled blueberries and beer.* The waiter seemed not to notice that my wife had been replaced by my student.

Watching Clara eat up Caroline's dessert gave me a pleasure similar to serving Jacob ice cream fifteen years before. Young people eating sweets made me happy.

"Did you always want to teach?" she asked. "I can't imagine you doing anything else."

"I wrote," I said. "I wanted to write."

"Write what?" she said.

"Translations and poems. Essays. I'm embarrassed to admit it, but novels too. Novels mostly."

"Embarrassed?" she said.

"I guess not," I said.

"What happened?" she said.

"That's not very nice," I said. I laughed it off. "I needed a job. I couldn't make rent as a writer. Mr. Madison remembered me from Princeton and offered me a steady salary. I've always loved teaching."

"I get that," she said. "Teaching is important."

"Initially it felt like a cop-out," I said. "But not anymore. Now it feels like the best way I could spend my life."

She took a last bite.

"How did Caroline feel?"

"I was already a teacher when I met her."

"She loves you because you're a teacher?" she said.

"Because?" I said.

"People love people because of things," she said.

"What happened in San Francisco?" I said.

"I couldn't make rent as an entrepreneur. I wanted to farm."

"Clara," I said.

"Mr. Keating," she said.

"Coffee or tea?" the waiter said.

"Coffee, please, decaf," I said. "Clara?"

"I'm fine with water," she said.

(December 2019, continued)

Whenever I think about my early attempts at writing, I'm reminded of this old joke:

> *A writer died and was given the option of going to heaven or hell. She decided to check out each place first. As the writer descended into the fiery pits, she saw row upon row of writers chained to their desks in a steaming sweatshop. As they worked, they were repeatedly whipped with thorny lashes.*
>
> *"Oh, my," said the writer. "Let me see heaven now."*
>
> *A few moments later, as she ascended into heaven, she saw rows of writers chained to their desks in a steaming sweatshop. As they worked, they, too, were whipped with thorny lashes.*
>
> *"Wait a minute," said the writer. "This is just as bad as hell!"*
>
> *"Oh, no, it's not," replied a voice. "Up here, the work gets published."*

(August 2012, continued)

"You won't tell me *anything* about college? Or at least about Dalton?" I said.

"Dalton was an offensive place full of offensive people," Clara said. "You were right. I should have listened to you. I hated everyone."

"You missed Jacob," I said.

"I missed Jake, but I resented him too." She paused, looking off to the side, in the direction of the closest window, which showed only darkness. "I loved him," she said.

After a few seconds she seemed to collect herself and gave a self-conscious laugh. "Anyway, it was eighth grade."

"Eighth grade is important," I said.

"No, it's not," she said.

Then she turned and looked at me.

"Sorry," she said. "Of course it is. That's not what I meant."

I swirled my pickled blueberries into the beer-flavored ice cream. I slid my chair back and crossed my legs at the thigh.

"So in the end you wish you hadn't gone to Dalton?" I said.

"Mr. Keating," she said. "I don't care about Dalton."

The staff was in no rush to kick us out. Clara knew many of them. I was worried my decaf was actually regular. It tasted too deep and complex to be decaf, and if I didn't sleep that night I'd get sick, which at my age meant a few days lost. But I didn't say anything about the coffee. I tried to center myself in the moment. To make the most of Clara. As we talked, we watched the other diners finish their meals and then the waiters and busboys (though there must be a new and more appropriate term than *busboys* for the male and female adult employees who clear plates off tables) begin to clean up. Music was replaced by the machine-gun chirping of crickets and the hoots of owls.

"You have to tell me something about your life," I said.

Clara told me about a farm where she'd interned after leaving the tech world and about a Professor Plum—Jeff Plumolinsky—who ran it. His mission was clean, sustainable farming, but it was also to "spread the good word." That's what his disciples said. As far as I could tell, Clara counted herself as one.

Professor Plum reminded her of me, she said.

I couldn't understand why. From her description of him, he sounded a bit like a cult leader in overalls and a work shirt, trailed by reverential interns obsessed with "the philosophical problems of drip irrigation"; he was pioneering some new kind of "wicking" system I couldn't follow. "Professor Plum." Absurd.

"How did he remind you of me?" I said.

She thought for a moment. "He was kind. And," she added with a hint of a smile, "performative. He saw I wanted to learn and could learn quickly."

It was Professor Plum, I discovered, with not a little jealousy, who forever changed the course of Clara's life. Clara, *my* student. And what had he done that was so monumental to Clara, such a dramatic inflection point in her trajectory? Professor Plum had taken Clara on her first visit to a factory farm.

Clara didn't want to talk about Dalton, Swarthmore, or Silicon Valley. She wanted to talk about "Cowshwitz." Cowshwitz. It was a god-awful place, and I couldn't tell exactly why Professor Plum took her there. To indoctrinate her further? To link her to him?

As she told me about the ride there, the smell, her "gagging in the car" and the "physical wave of filth" that hit her when she opened the door, I tried to accept her at face value as an adult who'd gone through a spiritual awakening. She'd visited the depths of hell. One hundred fifty thousand cattle gathered from ranches all over the West. She saw the suffering, literally breathed decay and death into her lungs, purged, and emerged a different person, carrying the suffering away with her but at the same time somehow having been cleansed of it.

She talked with sincerity and passion. She was still, but confident. She didn't use her hands or shift her weight. I couldn't entirely accept that this woman in front of me was Clara. I mean, she looked and acted like Clara, and I knew she was the same Clara I'd met at the birthday party when she was five and whom I'd taught a decade later. Her eyes were the same. Blue and bright. And her brain was as sharp as ever. Sharper, even, if that was possible. My problem was that kids can do anything, become anyone, go in any direction. They have potential in a way adults do not. All kids have it, and Clara'd had it more than anyone. She could have been an astronaut, the president, a novelist, a teacher. But she had to choose one thing. Which was difficult for me to accept. Not because there was something wrong with sustainable farming, but because it excluded so much else.

Maybe if I'd been in touch with her all those years, her choice wouldn't have felt so stark. That out of the million possible Claras, there was only this single one left. And she had already done so much. And she was still young. And she was talking about maximum impact—reversing the horror of our whole system of sustenance through her own moment of revelation. It was powerful. Moving, even. There was nothing wrong with any of it. I was proud of her.

(August 2012, continued)

But there was something in me while I was listening to her that was tinged with sadness. And here I sit feeling the same or a different sadness, writing about Clara and tortured livestock and Professor Plum.

I tried to explain earlier why I'm not writing about myself. The next obvious question is, why am I not writing about Caroline either? When she's the love of my life? When she is real, spends every day with me, takes care of me, is the only person to whom I've ever really mattered? You say my mother, but she didn't know me. She knew some child. Caroline is the one. So why aren't I writing about her? Why, instead, am I recounting Clara's epiphanic hour at Cowshwitz? Shouldn't I be writing about Caroline's childhood upstate; her father's alcoholism; her first marriage; her talent for painting and piano; the birth of her son; how I courted and won her?

I believe it is considered unsophisticated these days to quote Hemingway on literature or on life, but he was onto something when he put into the mouth of a character in *The Sun Also Rises* that if you talk about something, you lose it.

How do you describe a happy marriage? The first time Caroline and I got drunk together after closing at the bookstore. Or, even better, the first time she didn't charge me for a book. A glance at her collarbone. But all that is courtship, not marriage. Writing about the courtship after twenty-five years of marriage is superficial, paltry, unworthy. And our marriage is too subtle.

How can I write about Caroline and everything she's ever done for me and with me and have that not be a disappointment to her? I couldn't bear it. I can't even write her an anniversary card. To put my feelings for her into writing: *I love you. You make my life worth living.* That's not exactly right. *I love you. You are my life.* That's closer. *My life is yours.* That's closer still.

Tolstoy wrote that all happy families are alike, but every unhappy family is unhappy in its own way. That part about happy families never felt true to me. Better was his line about how loving someone meant loving them just as they were, not the way you wanted them to be. Caroline is the only person I've ever known to love me as the adult I am. Which is how I do my best to love her. But try to put that into a scene. Use the camera method. Show her taking a washcloth off the stack, warming and soaping up the water. Rolling me into the bathroom, undressing me as a parent undresses a child. Or as a child undresses a doll. Dipping the cloth in the water. She feels my body shiver even though I can't feel it.

* * *

Mark Twain wrote something about marriage making two fractional lives a whole, which seems true. Enid understood what Twain was getting at when she talked about needing to create a family in order to be happy. But that wholeness is not the stuff of literature, or, if it belongs in literature, it's for sonnets, not novels. Marriage—when its participants are healthy, at least—is the stuff of daily life. The stuff that matters: The lentil soup. The "Do you want to shower first or should I?" The bad nights' sleep. The glass of water. The taste of her mouth's kiss. My life with Clara had a plot. My life with Caroline was something bigger, more amorphous, shapeless, and all-encompassing.

(August 2012, continued)

"Well, why come to me?" I asked Clara. "Why not ask Professor Plum to vouch for your whereabouts?"

I thought she would answer that Professor Plum was too far away or too connected to the movement to avoid suspicion or maybe just too dead.

But instead Clara said, "Because I always come to you."

"The only advice I've ever given you is not to attend Dalton," I said, "and you didn't listen."

"You've protected me my whole life," she said.

I didn't understand.

"With the crystals at Jake's mom's place. The cell phone at lunch. It was why I called you when I was pregnant in high school."

"What do you mean?" I said.

"I'd just found out," she said. "I invited you to that scholarship dinner wanting your help. I just needed someone to talk to. But Aaron was there, and for some reason Mr. Madison showed up too, and you seemed... I don't know. You seemed distracted." This was a different kind of remembering and recounting. The story about Cowshwitz she'd told a million times. This was unrehearsed. She was trying to piece together the truth. "But it was fine. I just went to Planned Parenthood and took care of it. It was easy. In fact, I felt proud not to have told you or anyone else about it. I did it by myself. It made me feel strong."

"My God, Clara, I'm so sorry," I said. "I could have helped. I could have gone with you."

"It was easy," she repeated. "I handled it."

"It couldn't have been easy," I said.

"I'm telling you," she said. "It was just physical pain."

"I knew there was something unusual going on that day," I said. "I should have checked in with you again."

"It's okay. I had — " She stopped.

"What?" I said.

"I had Jacob. That night after I did it, I started sleeping in his bed sometimes. I needed him. And I could tell he needed me too."

"Even when you two weren't together?" I said.

"In college once, I tried to go further, and he stopped me. He said we could do that, he wanted to do that, he wanted that, but that needed to be separate. That's not what this was."

"I'm sorry," I said.

"I don't want you to be sorry," she said. "About anything." She leaned across the table, took my hands in hers, and looked at me. Into me. The look in her eyes could have powered a city. "I know you feel like you've done important work," she said. "And you have. But help me now, and you'll be a part of something bigger than you ever imagined possible. In my new work, I'm remembering what it means to have community. I've never really had community before. Or not since you, Enid, and Jacob. And that was family, not community. You three are the only ones who never wanted anything from me other than to let you love me. I never stopped loving Jacob. I just put myself first. I used him for a bit but never stopped loving any of you."

She told me she was asking me to join her. She told me it would be the most important thing I'd ever done. She told me to say I had been with her in New York City on a certain date in May.

(August 2012, continued)

I hesitated. Clara saw me wavering.

"What?" she said.

Pain is bad. We don't want living things to suffer. Certainly not in the billions. But also... I admit it, I don't really care about either the suffering animals or the people who work in the slaughterhouses. I don't know why I don't care. It makes me feel terrible. Or at least, it makes me think I should feel terrible.

But these people and animals are an abstraction to me.

Back when I was able to chew and swallow moo shu beef, I ate moo shu beef because it gave me pleasure. And perhaps if I had to murder (or even smell) the cow, its beef would no longer give me pleasure. Or a better way of putting it is that if I had to murder the cow myself, my displeasure in murdering the cow would be more powerful than the pleasure of eating the moo shu beef. Especially if I had to torture that cow first or watch it be tortured. Preventing a single animal from suffering was totally worth my not eating it, but would my not eating animals actually prevent a single animal from suffering, or was the system of factory farming so large and driven by such disparate forces that my abstention — even mine along with thousands of others', tens of thousands of others' — would have no effect at all?

So I was left in a position where I wanted to eat meat, it was easy for me to eat meat, and my not eating meat wouldn't prevent any animals from being tortured and murdered. In all likelihood, the massive number of animals processed by factory farms over the course of my lifetime would remain exactly the same whether I boycotted meat or not.

I said as much to Clara, and to my surprise she replied, "I completely agree."

"So you're not a vegan?" I said.

"I'm a vegetarian. But I agree. Individual action — individuals caring about individuals — isn't enough."

I was scared for her and a little scared of her. But I understood now that this was — for the moment, at least — the logical purpose of her life. Her telos was to save the maximum number of lives, regardless of species.

"You can come to a meeting sometime if you want to see," she said. "If you want to join. All I *need* you for is one thing — for you to say I was with you that day. But it's not all I want you for. You are the best teacher I've ever had. Better than anyone at Dalton, Swarthmore; better than Professor Plum. You are a good man. And I want you to be a part of what we're doing. I want you to learn and then to teach. Our community needs teachers. Good people. And you can enter this different stage in your life. You can accomplish more with us in a month than you've done at St. George's in years." She blushed. Stammered: "I'm s-sorry. I'll stop. I don't mean to keep offending you. You've meant a lot to so many of us. You taught us how to write. To experience, to love literature. To work hard to achieve goals. That means something. But even so. Together we act on a magnitude, a scale many times larger than you've ever had access to. We don't only enrich lives. We save them."

"You think I'd fit in?" I said. It was meant to be a joke but I heard myself sound serious. Maybe I was serious.

"I don't know. Mr. Keating, I can't claim to really know you. But I want to know you better. Not as a teacher but as a friend. A real friend. From what I can tell, you care about life lived to its full potential. I know that. Can we start with your vouching for me once?"

"We can," I said.

(January 2020)

"In youth the years stretch before one so long that it is hard to realize that they will ever pass, and even in middle age, with the ordinary expectation of life in these days, it is easy to find excuses for delaying what one would like to do but does not want to; but at last a time comes when death must be considered." When jokes are not enough and it's time to create something lasting. I will be gone soon. Caroline soon after. Or maybe she lives another twenty years. That's still soon enough. And then what? Without a benevolent, omnipotent, omniscient God, I cannot count on a heaven where I will continue living or where we will reunite. Also, there's no guarantee either of us would get in. Caroline probably. Me, I give it a fifty-fifty shot. So what remains? My students' memory of a teacher they once had, this manuscript, and whatever I've helped Clara accomplish.

Caroline was reading to me today from Maugham's memoir *A Summing Up*, and when she hit that line about considering death, I stopped her, in awe. I don't cry very often, but I did at those words. I could have written them. I might as well have. Also, check out this passage from the same book, about writers: "We do not write because we want to; we write because we must...We must go on, though Rome burns. Others may despise us because we do not lend a hand with a bucket of water; we cannot help it; we do not know how to handle a bucket. Besides, the conflagration thrills us and charges our mind with phrases." How great is that? Don't come to us when Rome is on fire because (1) we don't know how to use a bucket, and (2) we're thrilled to watch Rome burn.

(August 2012, continued)

The morning after the dinner at the restaurant, I couldn't get out of bed. Same thing the morning after, and the one after that. I'd been living a routinized life: Sushi or lentil soup for dinner. Asleep by ten o'clock. My body wasn't ready for a late night and all that rich food. My soul wasn't ready for all that conversation. We stayed in our bed-and-breakfast for three days. Caroline went on walks or drove to the closest gas station to buy me saltines and Gatorade.

When I tried to explain the conversation I'd had with Clara, Caroline didn't understand. I don't mean it in the way that she's starting to be forgetful now. I didn't understand my conversation with Clara either. There was too much to understand. I was tired. She refused to vouch for Clara, as I'd known she would. But she couldn't control what I said, and she wouldn't contradict me unless directly asked. I didn't want to talk to anyone about it. I mean, I wanted to talk to Richy but it was too late for that, so after Caroline and I made it back to the city, I started going to Yankee games alone and talking to him in my head.

(October 2008)

Caroline and I were not regular consumers of financial news, so we didn't realize how serious the global financial crisis was or how distressing its results would be. Though we regretted allowing her son, Henry, to invest our meager savings in the NASDAQ years prior, it was for the most part paper profits we lost. I knew that Richy had been gambling heavily and feared that he was badly hit, but he was taking an administrative sabbatical in Thailand with his wife, Patty, giving her the six months away he'd always promised her, and he wasn't answering emails. It took a full two weeks after the market crash before I heard from St. George's chairman of the board that the school was ruined and Richy was dead.

I am not a business-minded man. In my memory, I seem to have mixed up the crash of 2008 and the Bernie Madoff scandal that soon followed. Caroline tells me that Lehman Brothers collapsed in September, and Madoff was arrested in December. Richy frequently boasted of his investments in "commodities" and "growth stocks" that he played around with on whim and insider whisper. That, to him, was gambling money, and he'd been winning. The safe money—his real savings—was with Bernie.

Richy and Madoff had been introduced to each other by Sandy Koufax. He thought they'd get along. They chatted briefly at an outdoor luncheon thrown by Sandy's business manager. Richy tried to arrange a follow-up meeting with Bernie. Bernie refused (that was his pitch strategy, as you've probably heard). Richy had to beg to get in, then sent him a few million to invest. Just as Bernie promised, the initial investment paid out 10.5 percent annually. A few years later, Richy convinced the board to invest half of St. George's endowment with Bernie. This was where Bernie made most of his money. Nonprofits, which functioned more like individuals than companies, didn't have the same fiduciary reporting requirements as large funds. The Elie Wiesel Foundation for Humanity lost $15.2 million, and Wiesel and his wife, Marion, lost their life savings. Richy had mentioned a few years earlier that he was making money alongside Elie Wiesel, and I'd asked if there was any chance he might beg Wiesel to talk to my class. I'd taught *Night* every year for two decades. Richy thought it was a grand idea, but nothing ever came of it. I include it here only to attest to the fact that in my small way, I too encouraged Richy to continue his association with Bernie.

Richy lost all of his own money and most of the school's.

To this day, Patty says it was a heart attack. There was no reason to challenge the family narrative.

A tasteful service. Excruciating. I should have spoken but I didn't. Several former students spoke. One talked about how Richy's attending his bar mitzvah made him really feel like a man for the first time. One spoke about how Richy encouraged her to apply for a Fulbright long after she'd assumed he'd stopped thinking about her.

And that was it. Very little mention of him followed at St. George's. There is no plaque or portrait there. A new head of school took over, Sarah Templeton, a PhD in history from Princeton with no interest in finances. She sometimes referred to me as her fellow Tiger.

I'm not sure why I have withheld the story of Richy's death until now. It doesn't belong here any more than it would have belonged chronologically. The truth is, I've never understood Richy's role in my life so I am unable to understand his death. He was the closest friend I ever had.

Over dinner at the restaurant upstate before Clara arrived, Caroline and I imagined how Richy would discuss each dish.

"The butter is *otherworldly*!" we said. "Have you *tried* the *tenderloin*!"

None of this was particularly funny but Caroline knew how difficult it was for me to talk about Richy, so she was always looking for small occasions where I could think about him without having a conversation for which I wasn't ready.

And I thought about Richy when I saw Clara. As much as he'd bet his finances on Madoff, he'd bet his legacy on her. And she'd quit on their dream. Or at least on his dream for her. Maybe he hadn't had the fortitude to recover.

* * *

"He loved you," Caroline said to me the night after the funeral, when I was crying and drunk on a bottle of Pappy Van Winkle that Richy had given me for my sixtieth birthday.

"No, he didn't," I said. "If he loved me, he would have called me first."

"People are complicated," she said. "And maybe it really was a heart attack."

"That's the best you can do?" I said.

I wish I'd asked Richy more about his childhood and told him more about mine. I wish I'd gotten to know his wife better. I wish I'd gotten to know her at all. I wish he could come visit me now and read me the books he'd never read but always wanted to. *The Razor's Edge* and Rousseau's *Confessions*. Everything I spent our years together telling him to read. He could read me the sports section. He could, with irony, watch *Friends* with me and discuss the various strengths and weaknesses of each character. He could argue that Joey was the mastermind behind the friends. I could tell him that *The Grapes of Wrath* and *Gatsby* are the two great novels of the Great Depression, but there is no great novel of the 2008 financial crash. He could mention *The Big Short*. I could tell him that *The Big Short* was nonfiction, not a novel. And that it made the horrors exciting, and I didn't like that angle from its author, Michael Lewis. In comedy, Richard Lewis, I like. Funnier than Jerry Lewis. They both suffer, but Jerry never seemed as aware of his suffering as Richard. "So we're ranking Lewises now?" Richy could say. In music—I'd continue—Huey Lewis was a genius, Jerry Lee Lewis highly overrated. The best two Lewises were Carl and John. And as fast as Carl ran, John takes the cake. Did you know he coined the phrase *good trouble*? Said something like "Never be afraid to get into good, necessary trouble." Back to writing: C. S. Lewis might be the worst Lewis. Even worse than Michael. Those Narnia books are just begging to have their cheeks pinched and heads patted. They are the cutesiest books ever written. The best Lewis writer is Sinclair. But still, if I had to choose one Lewis overall, it'd be John.

I wish Richy were alive now to see me in this sorry state and not judge me or think less of me. He knew the way my brain worked then and he'd still know that now.

Here's a story Richy and I laughed about. This was his favorite story, I think. His favorite joke. He told some half version of it to me at a Yankee game and then we watched YouTube clips of Mickey Mantle and Billy Martin telling it in various interviews. I leave it here for you, for him:

> *Billy Martin had such success managing the Rangers one season that Texas ownership rewarded him with a brand-new Winchester Model 70.*
>
> *So, first chance he had, Billy called Mickey Mantle to go out hunting.*
>
> *"I know a guy with acres of land out by Eagle Mountain Lake," Mickey said. "He's a doctor and an old friend, and I'm pretty sure he'll let us hunt on his land. It's far from here, but I bet he'll let us."*
>
> *"I don't care how far it is," said Billy. "I'm just desperate to go deer hunting with my new rifle."*

So Mickey and Billy drove all the way out to Eagle Mountain Lake. They parked on the side of Mickey's friend's farmhouse.

"Now, you just hang tight," said Mickey. "I'll get the go-ahead from my friend, and then we'll get down to hunting."

Billy sat in the passenger seat while Mickey got out of the car and knocked on his friend's front door.

The doctor was surprised to see his famous pal. "Hey, Mickey," he said, "what're you doing all the way out here?"

"I'm here with Billy Martin. He's just desperate to go hunting on fine land, and I told him yours was the finest."

"It'd be an honor to have you two out here," the doctor replied. "Just leave the car where it's parked and head on through the barnyard to that path to the woods."

Mickey shook the doctor's hand and turned back toward Billy.

"But, hey, Mick!" shouted the doctor. "Now that I think of it, can you do me a favor? On your way out through the barnyard, you won't be able to miss an old mule standing there by a red oak. Can you do me a big favor and shoot that mule?"

Mickey shook his head. "Come on, Doc," Mickey said, "we haven't got any interest in shooting an old mule. Billy and I came down here to hunt deer."

"Please, Mick? You'd be doing me a helluva favor," said the doctor. "Over the past few weeks I've tried to do it myself, but I just don't have it in me. That mule has been around for twenty-some-odd years, and he hasn't been able to work a

lick in the past ten. I'm going to have to have him put down anyway. You'll really be doing me a big favor."

"Fine," Mickey said, "I'll shoot your mule."

As he headed back to the car, Mickey decided to play a joke on Billy.

Mickey acted like he was furious. He yanked the door open. "Get me my gun!" Mickey said, as angry as Billy had ever seen him.

"What's the problem?" Billy said.

"We traveled half a day to go deer hunting, and now my friend says we can't go hunting on his property. You know what I'm going to do?" Mickey said. "I'm going to shoot the man's mule." Mickey took out his rifle and loaded it.

Billy grabbed Mickey's rifle. "Jesus, Mick, stop that. I know you're angry, but there will be police involved. The Texas Rangers won't want me ending up in jail."

"Let go of my rifle," Mickey said. Mickey pulled it away from Billy and rushed out to the barn. Billy followed.

Bang!

Mickey shot the mule in the head, and it dropped hard to the ground.

But then: Bang! Bang! Bang!

Mickey spun and spotted Billy with his gun. "Billy, what are you doing?"

"I got three of his cows too!"

(September 2012)

A woman from the FBI called, and I told her Clara had been with me in New York City that day. That we'd read together and watched the Yankees on TV. In actuality, Clara had never been to my apartment, but if she had visited, I'd like to think that's what we would have done. The agent thanked me and said she'd follow up with more questions but never did.

(October 2012)

Clara and I often spoke on the phone after that. A few times a week, I'd chat with Enid or Clara while Caroline napped or read. Caroline still managed the bookstore, kept up on all the latest book buzz. She recommended books to customers. Sometimes on weekends I'd linger by a bookshelf to hear her advise a high-school girl or middle-aged man on what to read and why. I've lived a blessed life.

Enid and I reminisced about SoHo in the days when art galleries proliferated. She told me she was worried about Jacob: Too much work. Not enough time with his wife. No kids in sight. Enid wanted a grandchild. She was envious of Caroline. Not because of me. She couldn't stand the thought of living with me for another minute of her life, she said. Jacob and Skye were busy, I said. Restaurants were notoriously difficult to run, and wasn't Skye a doctor? I told her to give it time. She told me she wanted a grandchild.

* * *

Clara told me about her growing community. At first it was nice to see her using her mind. Then I was intimidated by it. By her. She imagined an international network of cells that shared information but not names or specifics. If you haven't heard about the bombings by now, they were spaced out every six months or so for over five years. The costs were paid by the insurance companies. Insurance companies did raise fees, and those fees were passed along to consumers, who were asked to feel sorry for the factory farms, slaughterhouses, and processing plants. Clara's plan made sense, in theory. Disrupt factory farms by damaging property, which would make insurance fees skyrocket. Companies wouldn't be able to afford the overhead and would shut down or at least change the way they handled the animals. No humans would get hurt. But the companies would be pushed and prodded.

In reality, the principal public debate was over whether the participants in these actions were terrorists. One cell was infiltrated and prosecuted under a terrorist statute. Though some callers to *The Brian Lehrer Show* disagreed, conventional wisdom was that the activists were using terrorist tactics, so they were terrorists. This seemed like an absurd use of the term *terrorists* to me. Terrorists murdered people. Clara did everything she could to avoid human injury. Still, I told Clara I didn't want to know specifics. She said she understood, though she must have intuited my interest.

(March 2013)

I received the call on a Monday evening. Caroline and I were drinking beer and eating moo shu beef. *Jeopardy!* was on in the background. Caroline picked up, listened, and handed me the receiver. It wasn't Clara who called. It was a woman who sounded older. My age. She told me where to meet. What to bring. I didn't ask questions. It felt like a game. I hadn't played a game in decades. It felt as if we were playing at being spies. I'd just received my secret mission.

Caroline and I discussed it that evening over ice cream.

"I'd have to fly there, pay for it myself. And sleep in a motel. I don't want to leave you alone."

"You should go," Caroline said. "It's clear you want to. You don't need my permission."

The new head of school didn't act like my boss. Sarah Templeton knew how close Richy and I had been. She was waiting me out, desperate for me to retire. I was at the top of the pay scale, and she could hire four, maybe five associate teachers for the lower school the moment I hung up my Russian fur hat. I told her I needed a sub for the rest of the week. She asked me to email assignments and forward along any PDFs.

I flew from LaGuardia to Omaha Eppley, checked into the motel under the name I'd been told to. I was very anxious. At each stage, I was anxious about the next one. I had been battling fatigue from a recent virus and didn't want to embarrass myself. It's funny, looking back, that I was less scared of being caught than I was of embarrassing myself.

I paid for the motel room with cash. I'd never been to Nebraska before. Did you know that there's not a single MLB, NBA, NFL, or NHL team in the state? (Did you know almost half of US states—twenty-four of fifty—don't have a big-four team?) I saw some Broncos memorabilia in the airport. A few Kansas City Chiefs T-shirts. Mostly college gear.

I hadn't known anything about Nebraska. Before my trip, I looked it up. Not many people live there, and those who do live in Lincoln or Omaha. Outside of those cities, there are farmers. Nebraska, home of the US Meat Animal Research Center, has more people working in cattle slaughter than any other state.

At the appointed time, a white van picked me up from the motel's parking lot. There were four women and a man already in the van, and another man got in with me. The driver told us not to say our names or give any other identifying information. These folks were organized. Though I was very tired, the atmosphere in the van was pleasant. When the driver turned to check her blind spot, I saw her see me clearly for the first time. For a second, she froze. She was JuliaPaige, her blond hair only slightly darker than when she'd been in eighth grade. JuliaPaige Peres! Had she and Clara been in touch the whole time? We listened to Tom Petty. "Won't Back Down." "Free Fallin'." "American Girl." I'd never realized how great Tom Petty was. Some moments call for sincerity, and this was one of them. I was proud to be able to volunteer the information about the lack of professional sports teams in Nebraska. We drove for an hour or so on a large, mostly empty highway that cut through grasslands. When the Tom Petty CD ended, JuliaPaige played it again from the beginning.

We pulled up at a former firehouse. It looked abandoned. Another van had parked there and was waiting for us. There were sixteen of us, total. Clara in charge. She looked just like she had at dinner. Short hair, heavy sweater. But her blue eyes were more focused. The people in that van must have been waiting for some time, because as soon as we got out of ours, Clara told everyone to gather around. She counted us, considered options. Decided. Gave orders. No one else seemed to know her personally. But then again, I didn't indicate that I knew her, and neither did JuliaPaige, so maybe it was the same with others. She asked if anyone needed to relieve themselves, and a few of us did; we went behind the firehouse.

"Circle up, everyone," Clara said.

Clara spoke softly, so we had to lean in. If people were anxious, they didn't show it. Ten women and six men. All white. All dressed in plain-colored clothes. I'd checked the weather before I left. Though it was March, the temperature was low enough that I could see my breath, and there was a 50 percent chance of rain. I wore my Russian fur hat and my big Scottish galoshes. Clara's boots were good working boots. The night before, I'd woken up gasping from a nightmare and was unable to get back to sleep. I started to feel anxious that I might not be able to perform what was asked of me. I took deep breaths. I didn't want to let Clara down.

"I'm going to hand out the papers now that will tell you where to go and what to do," she said. "If you have any questions, let me know. It's good of you to have come all this way. It means a lot to me, and to the world."

My arms felt stiff. Again I reminded myself to breathe.

I took my paper. My job was to stand watch at the exit ramp that cars might use to head in our direction. The van would drop me, and I would radio whenever I saw a vehicle turn off the road. I would provide information on what type of vehicle it was, the color, make, size. And send out an emergency alert if it looked like law enforcement or security. From the one question I overheard, I gathered that many of us were positioned leading up to the main building.

"What else can I tell you," Clara said. "We've been assured the slaughterhouse will be empty. There are no animals there, so no security to protect them. You all can also know now," Clara said, "that six simultaneous operations are active currently in the country. The goal is to cripple the slaughtering of cattle at six of the ten largest operations. Tomorrow will be a bad day for the industry."

My vision blurred. I tried to take deep breaths. JuliaPaige and another young woman were holding me up. I kept trying to tell them to go ahead without me. That I didn't want to ruin this for Clara. That I didn't want to get in the way.

(March 2013, continued)

I don't know who drove, but Clara held my head in her lap. She chose me over her work. *Work* is a silly word for it. Her terrorism. Her benign terrorism. Her attempt to remake the world. I felt the embarrassment of a teacher or parent being cared for by a student or child. But embarrassment was soon replaced by tenderness and then something more powerful. She stroked my hair and told me she remembered everything I'd ever taught her.

A preposition was "anywhere a mouse can go."

A sentence that used every part of speech was *But* (conjunction), *gosh* (interjection), *you* (pronoun) *are* (verb) *really* (adverb) *in* (preposition) *terrible* (adjective) *trouble* (noun).

I am, I thought. *I am.*

I'd taught her well.

I didn't see Caroline and Clara together.

They'd switched places. One was with me and then the other one was. Clara back to her attempts to remake the world. Caroline back to me.

(September 2014)

A year and a half later, neither Jacob nor Clara had visited, but Skye came as soon as I started seeing guests. She'd asked to come sooner, but I'd met her only that one time at Enid's home for the engagement party, and I wasn't ready to be around anyone other than medical providers, family, and occasionally Christophe Lejeune. It's possible one or two others came by too. Of the incidents after the stroke, my memory grows hazy.

When Skye visited, I hadn't yet figured out how best to interact. I need to be able to see both screens as I write, and there's no room next to my rather large chair. My stepson, Henry the inventor, has since rigged up a projection machine that can be seen by my guests. But when Skye came, I didn't have it set up yet, so I mostly listened. That was okay, because she mostly wanted to talk.

* * *

She'd come because during their marriage counseling before their separation and then divorce, she had accused Jacob of avoiding any discussion about his past with Clara.

"I haven't talked about Clara with anyone in years!" Jacob had said.

"I don't believe you," Skye said.

"Only Mr. Keating! And that was just once, drunk, and I regretted it."

So after their relationship ended and she was free to do what she wanted, she wanted to talk to me. Spend some time with the one person who truly understood the extent to which she'd never had a chance.

I remember conversations I had in my forties and fifties much better than those since the stroke, but I've retained the gist of what Skye said during her visit, and I remember her attitude. She was a detective. A serious woman looking for clues that would exculpate her from what she understood as her failure to stay married.

She sat on the couch across from my chair. My two screens, one beside the other, were separated at the time by two feet or so, which framed her nicely. She looked nothing like the young fiancée from a few years before. She was more attractive now. Older. More honest in her appearance. Gone were the red lipstick, eye makeup, and black hair dye. Her tattoo was covered by a pale blue sweater that looked like cashmere. In her early thirties, she was a mature woman. Beautiful, really. Almost done with her radiation oncology residency. She had a new boyfriend and was happy. She hadn't been this happy since the early days of dating Jacob. Her new boyfriend had a son with whom she was starting to get along.

* * *

Skye talked. I nodded and nodded. I am a great nodder. The world's best, perhaps. I have full vertical control over my head and neck. When nodding, I appear almost normal. Caroline tells me my face relaxes when I nod. Nodding is what I do best, and it's rare that folks come to me for affirmation, so I was thrilled to show off. Caroline interrupted to ask if I needed to rest. I growled at her. I'm not as good at growling as I am at nodding, but they both understood. They laughed. Skye asked me questions, gave me information, and I nodded.

Skye hadn't heard the name Clara until she and Jacob were engaged. And it was Enid who'd first spoken it.

Skye and Jacob had moved in together the year before they got engaged, and Skye had attended all sorts of birthday and holiday celebrations with Enid, but she didn't feel as though she knew her well. Skye felt that Enid was keeping her at a distance, and though now Skye blames that distance on Enid's knowledge of her son's enduring love for Clara, at the time Jacob always said, "That's just my mom. She's distant by nature. She only really cares for her work."

But everything changed after the engagement. Skye loved the real Enid. They started hanging out, just the two of them. They saw matinees together. Musicals. Who knew Enid loved musicals? Skye loved Enid quickly and nearly as much as she loved Jacob. She'd always wanted her parents to be more like Enid. Self-sufficient. Interested in the world beyond driving directions and investments and who was applying to the golf club.

* * *

And then one day, the three of them sat around Enid's dining-room table. The wedding would be very small, so for the engagement party at Enid's apartment, the plan was to invite friends of Enid's who'd like to celebrate the couple but wouldn't make the final cut.

I was on the list for the engagement party. So was Harold Hopkins. Richy and Szilvia had already passed away.

"Do you want Clara on this list or at the wedding?" Enid said.

"Neither," Jacob said.

"I know she most likely won't come," Enid said. "But shouldn't you still invite her to something?"

"Who's Clara?" Skye asked.

"No way!" Enid said. Enid was being playful. "You haven't told her about Clara?"

"Should I be worried?" Skye said, trying to be playful too, though the truth was that she had never stopped worrying about her relationship with Jacob, even after he proposed to her, even now that they were planning their wedding. She wasn't a worrier by nature. That Jacob made her worry meant he made her care. It was part of what she loved about him.

"Jacob, shame on you!" Enid said, which Skye maintains was the moment from which they never recovered.

Enid was excited to discuss Clara, but she should have known not to introduce her into their lives. It probably wouldn't have mattered, but there's a chance the marriage could have survived Clara if Jacob had been more intentional about helping Skye understand.

"Clara Hightower," Enid said.

"That name rings a bell," Skye said.

"She had her fifteen minutes of Silicon Valley fame when we were just out of college," Jacob said. "She also happened to be my first girlfriend. We've talked about her."

"Have we?" Skye said to Jacob, expecting to hear that Clara was some long-ago girl who'd gotten away and he never mentioned her because he never thought about her.

"We'll talk about it later."

Two weeks later, Skye was still waiting. She very badly wanted him to bring it up. She'd googled Clara, read all the articles and watched all the clips. If Jacob brought Clara up, it might be natural. If Skye did, it would both suggest her jealousy and prove that he was purposely avoiding the topic. If he was avoiding it, she was right to be worried. He was avoiding it. She was right to be worried.

Another week later the two of them were out at dinner. Café Gitane in NoLIta. Jacob loved the couscous, and the restaurant was about the size and shape of the spaces he was looking at leasing. Window in the front, a small bar and kitchen to the right, seating for thirty, if that. He was in a good mood, drinking beer and eating couscous. Discussing the benefits of stools (more could fit in a space) versus chairs (more comfortable). Maybe a combination of both, he said.

Skye didn't want to ask, but even more, she didn't want to live as she was living. "Tell me about Clara," she said.

"There's nothing to tell," he said.

"Please," she said.

"Clara was my first girlfriend. You remember. I told you I lost my virginity to her in eighth grade."

"You said it was to some girl in your building. You didn't tell me she was famous."

"She wasn't famous when we were dating. I was fourteen years old. Are you jealous?" he said. "You're jealous! She lived in my building and went to St. George's with me. We dated for the last half of eighth grade. She broke up with me. There's nothing else to say. I think she works in farming now. She's a farmer."

"You lost your virginity to a farmer!" Skye said, still thinking she might turn Clara into a joke between them.

"She was thirteen. She was just a kid."

"I know that," Skye said.

"Sorry," Jacob said and began talking about the restaurant again, how he would offer a variety of small plates and just a few entrées.

Skye and Jacob got married, bought a place together in Brooklyn, opened Jacob's restaurant, worked different hours. Young people think that marriage concludes a story. That when two adults, after whatever vicissitudes you like, are at last brought together, they have fulfilled their biological function, and interest passes to the generation that is to come. But marriage is no more an end than birth is.

"You've made me so happy today," Skye's father said at the wedding. "I never thought I could be as happy as this." Skye's father wasn't unintelligent, and he certainly wasn't cruel, but he was wrong. Marriages must be fought for and endured. Childbirth must be fought for and endured. Skye would have to go to work every day and fight for her marriage and fight for any children she might have. And now she had to do it all with the pressure of knowing that if some part of her life didn't work out — if she was sad or sick or alone — she'd break her father's heart.

* * *

A few months before Clara invited us to that restaurant upstate, her parents died, and Enid told Jacob he had to attend the funeral. I don't recall if it was for Clara's mother or father, but I'm left with the impression it was somehow for them both. Skye went with Jacob, hoping to meet Clara. Hoping to see she had nothing to fear. Only five people were there in a small, windowless room at a death chapel in the East Village: Enid, Jacob, Skye, and two strangers. The place smelled of permed hair. The only person who spoke was this guy who used to work out in a judo studio with Clara's mom before her health began to falter. No sign of Clara.

For a while, Skye thought the problem was their misaligned schedules. Jacob worked six nights a week until after midnight. Sometimes much later. Skye's rotations shifted, and she was always exhausted. But still, she tried to make time for them. On his day off, at least. But then he was too tired. He didn't want to go out to eat after spending all week at a restaurant. Stopped wanting to go on hikes, or to the beach, or to the park. He was too tired to think about having kids. Too tired to have sex. She was the one training to become a fucking doctor, and he was too tired to be married.

"Would you have been jealous if you were me?" Skye asked. I nodded. "I was jealous. I was confused. I didn't know if he was actually tired or sick or cheating or just thinking about Clara."

When confronted, Jacob acknowledged she was right to be upset. He hadn't been generous enough. He reprioritized the relationship. Even if it meant his missing an additional brunch and dinner service each week. He was the owner, but for most meals, he was also the general manager and sometimes the host or a server. It was a small operation and the smaller he kept his budget, the more he could spend on ingredients. On keeping the menu prices down. That one weekend day they spent together, Skye and Jacob started talking about having kids eventually, but not now, not yet, not while their schedules were so misaligned.

I nodded. This information wasn't mine to know, but what did it matter? Who was I going to tell?

She had his Gmail password and read his emails every day. Nothing was there. Just business orders. Job requests. Jokes from his friend Eric. She checked her email whenever she had a moment between patients. But no one sent her emails. And then she checked his. No one sent him emails either. One night at home, a year or so after they got married, Jacob was at the restaurant late. Skye poured herself a glass of wine, took a bath, got in bed, scrolled through Facebook on her phone, smoked a joint, and turned on the TV. She happened to be a Red Sox fan, but that's not a metaphor, it's real life, so don't read anything deeper into that. Lots of people have great marriages while rooting for rival teams. She watched the Red Sox game that happened to be on ESPN. The Red Sox were working the opposing pitcher deep into the count, and the game was only in the sixth inning at ten thirty. Only in the eighth at midnight. She grabbed her laptop. She checked her email and then his. It was right there. She muted the TV. After years of looking, she'd found it. She didn't know what it was yet. She boosted herself up on her pillow. Prepared herself. Turned off the TV. Put her wineglass on the night table. Sat up straighter. And focused.

Eric had responded, I don't know, man. Talk to her. You're spinning out of control on this. to Jacob's email from earlier in the day: Do normal married people feel this lonely when they're with their spouses? I don't know what to say. I feel like she's always waiting for me to say something. I never know what to say.

"It was just the same as keeping a journal," he'd told her when she asked, and he repeated it to their therapist. "Rather than bottle it all up with nowhere to put it, I wrote an email to my friend. I've never cheated. I've never thought about cheating. I just want you! I'm trying so hard. Talking to a friend seemed healthy to me. There is no difference between thinking these things and writing them down. Jesus, Skye, I'm lonely."

"I'm lonely too," she said.

"I know. You're right. I'm sorry. I married you. I asked to marry you knowing full well what our lives were going to be."

"What does that mean, *what our lives were going to be*?" she said.

"I don't know," he said.

How awful that must have been for them both.

"I love you," he said.

"Are you sure?" she said, just wanting to hear that yes, he was sure. Of course he was sure.

But I don't know how he answered. Skye paused for a moment at this point. My best guess was that by that time in our conversation, she had realized I couldn't provide whatever she was looking for. I nodded and did my best to contort my face into a sympathetic smile. Imagine looking for answers from — of all people — me.

When Skye picked up the story again, she said Jacob told her he thought they needed to be apart for some time. Skye agreed. She lived alone for a while. They found people online to go on dates with. Eventually they got back together. Things seemed like they might be getting better. They worked on finding time for each other. They programmed weekly date nights into their schedule in addition to that one weekend day per week. They went out to restaurants; they went to the beach, to the park. They traveled to Italy and Spain. They were happy again. Then something happened. He asked for a divorce.

(September 2014, continued)

Something happened? I know what happened. I had a stroke. Clara held my head in her lap on the way to the hospital. Clara called Jacob to tell him. To blame herself. Who else could she have told? Enid wouldn't have understood. Jacob did. He always understood. He told her it wasn't her fault. Jacob told her that I—Mr. Keating—would have done only what I thought right and best. My broken body brought them back together.

(August 2020)

Earlier I wrote about how causality creates meaning in fiction, but real life is more complicated. And that's true. It's impossible to know if my trip to Nebraska caused my stroke, but my stroke irrefutably led Clara to call Jacob. So although Clara and Jacob might have spoken again for any number of reasons and no one knows if Jacob and Skye would have stayed together if not for what happened to me, in this life with these inputs and outputs, my stroke is what precipitated that call.

(December 2014)

Clara and Jacob visited me together. Holding hands. That's the image I hold on to. The two of them on the beige couch where Caroline and I had spent our marriage reading. Her hand in his. They both wore jeans and sweaters. Both leaned toward me. When they left, they promised to come back soon. They didn't, but I don't blame them. It can be difficult for some people.

Christophe visits, and Enid sometimes. Henry, of course. Henry tries to see his mom as often as possible. And you remember my former student Kai, the one who read that poem at the Ember Land Fair? He visits all the time. Reads to me every Tuesday and Thursday. We watch baseball together. He has three kids now. He brought them over here once and put the baby on my lap. As I said, it's hard on a lot of people. It takes a lot of work to spend time with me. I understand.

Jacob and Clara invited me to their wedding up at her farm, and I planned to attend, but in the end I couldn't. I'd been feeling well enough in the months before, but then Caroline and Henry took me to the Met as a kind of practice run, and the stress — both physical and, I'm ashamed to admit, psychological — of leaving the house for longer than my usual thirty-minute push around the block meant I couldn't focus for weeks. My blood-oxygen level plummeted. I needed a spell at the hospital. All sorts of difficulties not worth describing here. So the wedding was a no-go.

But we sent a gift. A bound copy of the Ember Exam.

In their thank-you note, they told me they had it up on their mantel. I like to think of them around a fire, the two of them home after a long day of work, him reading, her tending to the last of the chores on the farm. Or him cooking her dinner. I like thinking about him cooking her dinner.

That day they visited together, before their wedding, which I couldn't attend, they told me about how he proposed. I sat in my chair and looked at them. Caroline sat beside me in her chair. They sat on our couch. They were young and full of gratitude. They were nervous. I don't remember all of it, but I found their presence touching. He was very tall, and she was young again. She was shaking with what at first I thought was nerves but soon realized was happiness. It was almost like we were two normal couples. They took turns telling us what happened.

(April 2013–November 2014)

A week after Clara returns to upstate New York from Nebraska, she calls Jacob. It's the first time they've spoken in years beyond a couple of sentences. And she tells him as much as she can. About my stroke. About what led to it. What she's been doing. How she convinced me to be a part of what she was building. How I seemed interested. How maybe she pushed me too hard.

Three weeks later, he takes the day off from work. He wears his best suit. French cuffs, tie clip, slicked-back hair. He's almost thirty-one. It's been ten years. He is tall, thin from smoking cigarettes. Let her rebuff him. He just wants to see her.

He put on a very little bit of expensive cologne. She won't care. She lives on a farm. It's preposterous, the cologne, but she'll think it's funny. That's the point. When she first called, it was to talk about me.

Skye's name and his marriage didn't come up. They hung up. A few days later, she texted a photo of her smiling. She looked like Clara. A bit paler than he remembered.

He gets his shoes shined. He's never sat in one of those shoeshine chairs before and the only ones he knows still exist are near Grand Central Station, so he takes the subway to Grand Central, then picks up the rental car and starts driving to the address she gave him. Her farm. She'd texted again. Told him she'd bought a farm. He texted that he was happy for her.

The second time they spoke after my stroke, it was he who called her, he who primarily spoke. About how he and I went out drinking after his engagement. She thought that was funny. He admitted to spending the whole time talking about her. They talked about his marriage and why she'd never gotten married. Hadn't been in a real relationship since that French guy in San Francisco. They talked for hours.

She talked about high school, college, getting famous, rejecting fame. He talked about watching her from afar, never getting over her, his marriage, his restaurant. They both talked about Enid. His mother and her mother in a way too. They worried about her. She was getting older. Everyone was. They talked about JuliaPaige and Eric and me. They talked about Ember Land and the Ember Exam and Clara the Archon and Richy and Szilvia and Mr. Hopkins and Bruce and me.

* * *

He listens to the music they listened to in high school. He listens to Madonna and Live and the Beatles. He smooths down his hair. The drive is less than three hours long. All this time he's been three hours from her. All these years.

She'll be out on the farm, probably. She'll smell like farming. He doesn't care. His shoes will get ruined. He doesn't care. What will they have to talk about? What does anyone talk about? Sports, the farm, dinner that night, breakfast, people they used to know. Her voice had sounded like her.

The third time they spoke, he told her he was unhappy. Lonely. Busy, but bored. She said that she was lonely too. She told him about her attempts to disrupt factory farming. He asked questions. Listened. Learned. They talked about what healthy farming was like, how he could use her produce in his restaurant. How one day they could start a restaurant together. They fantasized about her food in his kitchen. About the menu. The location. I don't remember everything. I'm hazy on the chronology.

Her driveway is short and her house is small. It's a prefab house but not a box like he expected. It looks like a little cottage, with a porch and a chimney. Black-tiled roof, white stucco walls. The chimney looks like real brick. The steps up to the stoop are level. He'd imagined something out of the future when she texted *prefab*. She didn't know if he'd ever see the place. She mentioned it in passing.

But now, looking at her prefab house, Jacob sees what appears to be a normal little house. With wide glass windows in black metal frames. The driveway is one car wide, and a car is parked right at the front steps of her house. A white Saturn sedan. If it's her car, it's a surprising car for her to own, but he doesn't know anything about her. He would have guessed a truck would be better for farming, but he doesn't know anything about farming.

"Hello!" he calls from the driveway. "Clara?"

No response. He's breathing weird. He takes a deep breath and stretches out the muscles in his face by making his mouth and eyes as small and then as big as they can go.

He expects there to be animals on the farm, because it's a farm, but there aren't any animal noises. Some birds off in the distance. It's April, and he is cold wearing only his nicest suit. He flattens his hair. Flexes his pecs. He's been working out lately; he started after he realized how skinny he'd become. Not that she'll care. He's trying to quit smoking.

"Hello?" he calls again. "Anyone home?"

For several years, Jacob emailed me frequently. Caroline printed them out and read them to me. He always wrote that Clara sent her best. They were doing well. They planned a few visits into the city to see me, but between the farm and my health, those visits never materialized. They were going to bring Enid with them. Sometimes Enid brought us food and helped Caroline with the cleaning. But Enid didn't get to see Jacob and Clara very frequently, so why would she want to spend the time she had with them looking after me? Jacob wrote that they were thinking about having a child.

* * *

He still might write emails, but we can no longer get into our email account. That's okay. I like to think of the two of them together out there with their restaurant and their brilliant little boy or girl climbing around the kitchen table and onto their laps. I should ask Caroline to ask Enid about that.

He walks to the front door of Clara's house, knocks, turns the knob. Brass. Unlocked. He wipes his feet. He lets himself in. Walks through the house. His mother's art is everywhere. It's like walking into a dream. A benign nightmare: Your ex-girlfriend's house is empty. She's still the love of your life. Your mother's sculptures are on the bookshelves; your mother's photographs are on the walls.

"Clara?" he calls.

Jacob keeps on walking straight, through a mudroom, past a washer and dryer. There's mud on the floor. And boots. He keeps walking, out of the house, into the fields. Not much is growing. He finds some asparagus. He fights the temptation to kick it like a soccer player might.

"Hel-lo-o?" he calls.

"Hello?" he hears back. "Is someone there?"

A few times, Jacob has run into someone he hasn't seen since they were kids, and that person, as long as he or she hasn't gained or lost a lot of weight or gone bald, always looks much younger to him than a stranger would at that age. Clara hasn't gained or lost a lot of weight or gone bald. She looks like she looked when she was five and when she was thirteen and when she was seventeen. She's thirty now.

"You look the same," she says.

"I was just thinking the same thing," he says.

"I can't believe you came," she says.

"Really?"

"Okay, I kind of knew you would. I was just wondering when. I mean, I hoped you would."

"May I kiss you," he says.

"Are you serious?" she says.

"I am," he says.

"You don't know me," she says.

"May I kiss you," he says.

"You may," she says.

"Will you marry me?" he says.

"Really?" she says. "Slow down."

He takes her hands in his.

"Will you?" he says.

"Probably," she says, "but slow down."

"I love you," he says.

The taste of her kiss is different from Skye's and anyone else's. It is right. She feels right and smells right. He doesn't need to pretend. She is perfect. Her lips are chapped. He has no idea if she is kind or funny or even beautiful. He starts to cry and she does too.

(February 2021)

It's been six months since I was last here. In this document, I mean. On the page. Six months and a couple of days. I've realized I'm not going to finish the novel. I had a few more chapters written, but I deleted them just now. I'll end with Jacob's proposal to Clara. It's fine, I think, as is. It's good enough, or at least as good as I can make it. You've been introduced to Clara, and that's what matters.

I have always lived so much in the future that now, though the future is so short, I can't get out of the habit. There are moments when I have so palpable an eagerness for death that I could fly to it as into Caroline's arms.

Caroline broke her hip six months and a couple of days ago. It was my fault. I knew she'd been forgetful, but I wanted the television turned to the baseball game on a different station. I knew she'd been having trouble managing more than one thing at a time. The Yankees were playing. It was a rebroadcast of a game from years before. As though anything matters less than a rebroadcast. Caroline was cooking us eggs. I'd been eating a lot of very soft scrambled eggs, and I was making a whining noise. It's the noise we agreed I'd make when I got frustrated. It makes her frustrated. It *made* her frustrated, I mean. It was a good noise with which to indicate frustration, and sometimes I liked her to feel for a moment some tiny percentage of the frustration I felt at all times. I confess to wanting her to share my pain. I confess it made me feel less alone.

She was cooking, and I should have let her be. Instead, I kept making that noise. She'd been forgetting things.

She'd forgotten the Yankees were playing, and as hard as I tried to indicate to her that I wanted the television on a different station, she wouldn't listen. *Friends* was on, but I can't stand *Friends* now. I've seen them all. All the episodes. As much as Richy disliked the show, we talked about it some, and it reminds me of him. Also, the characters are loathsome, selfish, casually homophobic phantoms. There's no real ambition to them, no real love. It's a hollow, insipid program. So I made my frustrated noise, which made her frustrated. I wanted to watch the Yankee game.

I have no way of knowing for sure, but what I think happened is that she burned her hand on the pan, which somehow caused her to fall. She must have been scared. She'd been increasingly scared, knowing something was off and not wanting to tell me for fear of how it might scare me. I didn't want to make her say it. And anyway, what would it matter? She'd soon forget the conversation. She forgot to eat sometimes, and more often, she forgot to feed me. I should have told someone—the occupational therapist or Enid or Christophe or, at the very least,

Henry—but I didn't. I was afraid they'd take her away from me. Even when she was forgetful, I loved her. I loved her more when she was the vulnerable one. When I got to see her vulnerable again. I wish I had told her that I loved her more at the end than at the beginning.

The point is, I made my frustrated noise, and she burned herself on the pan, and she fell. She broke her hip and never came home again. I couldn't visit her, which was for the best, I'm told, but I don't know why or how it could have been for the best. To avoid the risk of my catching something at the hospital? Would that have been so bad? Missing her was worse. Being cared for by a stranger and wondering if I'd ever see Caroline again. I never did. It turned out her bones were brittle. Bone metastases. Cancer. She'd had cancer for God knows how many years. No one knows how long it'd been metastasizing or where it started. She spent her life taking me to doctors' appointments but never went herself. I should have told her to go. I should have insisted. I miss Caroline. There's not a moment of a day when I don't miss her. She made my thoughts matter. She made me matter. She still does.

Henry visits as much as he is able. He tells me her memory was much worse in the weeks after her fall. Sometimes she thought I was dead. But Henry also says she often spoke of me as my old self, talking and writing. Teaching. He says it made her happiest to hear about me teaching.

I'm waiting now. I watch baseball. Judge and Stanton on the same team. The pitching staff needs work, but whose doesn't.

(February 2021, continued)

Caroline's astrological sign was Cancer, so it's ironic how she died.

She was eaten by a giant crab.

(This joke is funny because you expect the irony to be that her sign, Cancer, is the name of the disease that killed her. It's surprising to find out it's not the word that provides the irony but the symbol for Cancer, which is a crab. Also, people are rarely eaten by giant crabs.)

Acknowledgments

I wrote *The Optimists* in memory of Rod Keating. Mr. Keating was my seventh- and eighth-grade English teacher and then my mentor when I began teaching eighth-grade English. In his classroom, you felt it: the quiet conviction that teaching, in its highest form, could change everything.

Thank you to Trena Keating (unrelated), the best literary agent in the United States. Thanks as well to Gaby Mongelli for her brilliant editing and Jean Garnett for advocating for and helping shape an early draft. Thanks to Matthew Buckley Smith, Andrew Palmer, Rafael Yglesias, Andy Bragen, Crystal Finn, and Hilary Gifford. Thanks to Grace Church School, the model for all that's good about the otherwise entirely fictional St. George's. Thanks to W. Somerset Maugham for lending this novel the structure of *The Razor's Edge*. Thank you to Mom, Dad, Jamie, and Ella, of course and always. And last and most, thank you to Alex, Owen, and Sam. I love you three the world.

About the Author

Brian Platzer was the education columnist for *The Atlantic* and has written frequently for the *New York Times, The New Yorker, New York* magazine, and many other publications. He currently teaches and lives with his family in Brooklyn and Paris.

RAISING READERS

Books Build Bright Futures

Thank you for reading this book and for being a reader of books in general. We are so grateful to share being part of a community of readers with you, and we hope you will join us in passing our love of books on to the next generation of readers.

Did you know that reading for enjoyment is the single biggest predictor of a child's future happiness and success?

More than family circumstances, parents' educational background, or income, reading impacts a child's future academic performance, emotional well-being, communication skills, economic security, ambition, and happiness.

Studies show that kids reading for enjoyment in the US is in rapid decline:

- In 2012, 53% of 9-year-olds read almost every day. Just 10 years later, in 2022, the number had fallen to 39%.
- In 2012, 27% of 13-year-olds read for fun daily. By 2023, that number was just 14%.

Together, we can commit to **Raising Readers** and change this trend. How?

- Read to children in your life daily.
- Model reading as a fun activity.
- Reduce screen time.
- Start a family, school, or community book club.
- Visit bookstores and libraries regularly.
- Listen to audiobooks.
- Read the book before you see the movie.
- Encourage your child to read aloud to a pet or stuffed animal.
- Give books as gifts.
- Donate books to families and communities in need.

BOB1217

Books build bright futures, and **Raising Readers** is our shared responsibility.

For more information, visit **JoinRaisingReaders.com**

Sources: National Endowment for the Arts, National Assessment of Educational Progress, WorldBookDay.com, Nielsen BookData's 2023 "Understanding the Children's Book Consumer"